DARKMOOR

DARKMOOR

The Darkness Discovered

Matador
9 Priory Business Park,
Wistow Road
Kibworth Beauchamp
Leicester LE8 0RX, UK
Tel: (+44) 116 279 2299
Fax: (+44) 116 279 2277
Email: books@troubador.co.uk
Web: www.troubador.co.uk/matador

ISBN 978 1780880 419

British Library Cataloguing in Publication Data.
A catalogue record for this book is available from the British Library.

Typeset by Troubador Publishing Ltd, Leicester, UK

Matador is an imprint of Troubador Publishing Ltd

Printed in Great Britain by the MPG Books Group, Bodmin and King's Lynn

For Nathan, Connor, Eve and Isobel. Enjoy.
And for my husband, thank you for being you.

- Chapter One -

The Victorian Vicarage

Catherine sat gazing across the road her eyes transfixed on number 21, the Old Vicarage, which had stood empty for years. There was no escaping it as her front yard overlooked the decrepit ancient building. Perching herself a little higher on the old rickety wooden bench, the vicarage sent shivers down her spine. Somehow, Catherine was intrigued by its mystical charm.

'It's so beautiful,' Catherine thought to herself as the sunlight smiled upon it.

The history of that old Victorian vicarage was still a mystery to this day. Screams and painful wailings were often reported to erupt out of its sash windows and echo throughout the village, leaving the people of Filius fearful and suspicious about the Vicarage's dark past.

Buried underneath a carpet of ivy, the old ruin stood all alone on the west side of Acerbus Road. A row of terraced houses occupied the east side and swept around like a fort protecting its castle.

Although it had been left lifeless by all humanity it did, however, have one inhabitant, Clever Crow.

As Catherine's dad always quoted, "If men had wings and bore black features few of them would be clever enough to be crows."

The crow had occupied number 21 for over ten years, and had somehow become tolerant of its ghostly surrounding's. Clever Crow would trick innocent animals to come and play with him, but then would cruelly have them for his dinner. He seemed to feast on the fear of the other animals and when their bodies started to decay the crow would still go on devouring their skeletal remains.

Catherine would watch the crow for hours and she was convinced that he was watching her too. He positioned himself high upon the chimney stack just like one of the Queen's guards, guarding his own castle. His pure silky black coat shone majestically in the evening sun leaving Catherine completely bedazzled.

Unfortunately for Clever Crow, he was about to have his fortress invaded. The Old Vicarage, which had been left derelict and lifeless for over a decade, was about to be resurrected back to life.

As the sun died down from view, Clever Crow stretched out his mighty wings and flew gracefully out of sight. Crow was gone.

"Cathy! Cathy! Come on darling, your supper's on the table," Catherine's mum called.

"Yeah, Mum, I'm coming," Catherine vacantly replied.

The smell of fish and chips greeted her as she headed through the lounge and into the kitchen. Friday night was chippy night which Catherine relished.

"Where's Dad?" Catherine asked whilst setting the table.

"He has to work late darling, but never mind, his loss," her mum replied softly.

Sitting down to eat supper together Catherine's mum asked, "What were you doing outside? Watching that flipping crow I bet?"

Catherine turned towards her mum and smiled.

"Mother, why ask if you already know?" Catherine remarked sarcastically.

"Because, my darling daughter, you're becoming increasingly obsessed with that bird. Anyway, you do know the new neighbours are moving in tomorrow?"

"Yes of course I do. Everyone in Filius and beyond is talking about it. You never know they might have a house warming, so then we could." Before Catherine could finish, her mum abruptly interrupted, "No Catherine. You're never to visit that house, never. Do you understand, Catherine?"

"But Mum," Catherine pleaded.

"No, Catherine. Have you not seen the latest poster?" Mum asked placing the glossy paper on the table which read,

MISSING!!
HAVE YOU SEEN THEM?

Underneath the bold writing were two pictures then underneath them...

ISABELLA COLLINS (AGED 5) AND THOMAS COLLINS (AGED 7) WENT MISSING ON THE 16TH APRIL AT AROUND 5.30PM.

THEY WERE LAST SEEN PLAYING TOGETHER ON ACERBUS ROAD, FILIUS.

IF YOU HAVE ANY INFORMATION REGARDING THE DISAPPEARANCE OF THE TWO CHILDREN, PLEASE CONTACT THE LOCAL POLICE ON 01276 21 34 65.

Reading it sent a shiver through Catherine. The words started to blur as Catherine stared hard at the printed text.

"I don't know if that place has anything to do with the missing children, but I don't want you over there. And besides, all those horrible sounds that use to come out of there," Mum lowered her voice, "it's not a nice place please promise me, Catherine?"

With both their hazel eyes locked together, Catherine sensed the unexplainable fear which her mum had towards the vicarage. Taking a deep breath, Catherine conceded.

"Ok, ok I promise I won't go anywhere near the Old Vicarage, or speak of it again."

After finishing dinner, Catherine left her mum watching the television and went to her bedroom. Catherine listened to some music on her mp3 player hoping it would take her mind of the vicarage.

"Don't step foot in there, Catherine," she squeaked mimicking her mum.

"As if it was haunted or something, it's just a house."

Besides, Catherine was too inquisitive. She would have to find out who was moving in to such a 'strange' house. And of course, it was her duty she had to make sure the clever crow was still there, if nothing else.

From underneath her pillow Catherine pulled out her diary and sat down on the edge of her bed. She had written in it every day since her eighth birthday, and it was her most treasured possession.

30th April
Dear Diary,

Have had a good day today, I've been to school and we played netball at dinner time. I also had Art which was brilliant because we got to use a potter's wheel. Although somehow, I ended up getting some of the clay into my hair! Yuk, it was horrible trying to get it out. Emma couldn't keep her clay on the wheel, lol!

Glad it's Friday, bank holiday weekend too, brilliant!

Dad worked late again. Been doing that a lot recently, oh well, must just have lots of work to do, Mum doesn't seem bothered.

I am well excited to get new neighbours moving into the vicarage tomorrow, can't wait! Wonder who it's going to be? Must be a family, the place is to big for one person.

Mum went ballistic when I mentioned about going over to meet them, said I had to promise her not to go in. She forgets I am 10! Been waiting for ages to have a nosey round.

I love the Old Vicarage and that funny old crow. I feel happy, but sad. Happy someone is moving in, but sad because

I always thought one day I would live there, somehow.

Anyway going to go now and get some sleep, big day tomorrow and I want to look my best.

Good night.

Catherine closed her diary and placed it back beneath her pillow. The pink leather bound book was starting to age, but Catherine didn't mind. It was the one place she could be herself and truly express her feelings, it was her best friend.

Once she was ready for bed she switched off her light. The moon was still aglow in her bedroom, allowing her to have one final peep at the old Victorian vicarage.

Although her mum had overreacted earlier she was right about one thing. Catherine was obsessed with that unexplainable building. It had a grip over her that she could not break free of, and it pained her to think that after tomorrow it might never look the same again.

With that thought her eyes began to fill with tears. Catherine always thought that it would be her that would one day inject zest back into the old building.

★ ★ ★

Catherine awoke to the sound of her mum's voice bellowing throughout the house. She quickly jumped out of bed and lay quietly on the floor. Pressing her ear into the carpet, she just about made out what her parents were saying.

"What do you mean you have to go into work? For goodness sake, Pete it's Saturday, you never work Saturdays," her mum's voice was not the usual soft tone Catherine was used to, but more stern.

"I know," her dad's voice began, "But it's just a one off, if I get my work done today, then I can be off tomorrow and Monday with you and Cathy, don't be mad love," Catherine's dad said calmly trying to restore peace.

"Don't be mad," her mum said having none of it. "Don't be mad he says, oh I'm not mad dear, I'm flaming fuming!" Catherine's heart sunk in her chest and her stomach began to churn.

Peeling herself up from the floor, Catherine had heard enough and headed off downstairs.

Noticing Catherine stood in the doorway they both stopped talking and almost in sequence smiled at her.

"Morning love, did you sleep well?" her dad asked sitting himself down at the table.

Amazed at the fact they were both acting like nothing had happened, Catherine answered, "Yeah fine thanks, you?"

"Yeah I did once I finally got home," he said accompanied by a nervous chuckle.

His cheeky comment had only made Catherine's mum even angrier.

"Yes and your Father has got to go back into work again today! Don't you dear? Anyone would think with all this extra work on you were having an affair!"

"What?" Catherine gasped.

"What?" Dad repeated in astonishment at the accusation.

Catherine looked at her mum sharply, trying to digest her words. A lump formed in Catherine's throat as she just about managed to ask, "Are you?"

He too was now enraged as he rose to his feet, "No I'm flaming not! How could you think that, Julie?" her dad's voice filled the air around them as Catherine's mum turned her back on him. With no explanation to offer him, an awkward silence descended around the three of them.

Only the sound of breathing could be heard for what seemed like an eternity, and Catherine didn't know what to say. She stood frozen to her spot longing for something to break the silence, but nothing until,

"Beep, beep, beep!!"

Catherine's parents sat themselves back down at the table with only the sound of munching to be heard.

Hearing the beeping once more, Catherine turned to look out of the window and asked, "Who's being noisy?"

"It will probably be the new folk moving into number 21," her dad answered chomping on his cornflakes.

"Of course, it's today," Catherine remarked. "I can't believe I forgot," she shouted with excitement.

Darting back through the kitchen, then the lounge and finally up the stairs to her bedroom.

"What about your breakfast?" her mum shouted after her.

"Breakfast can wait!" Catherine called back as the excitement spilled out of her.

Catherine had one thing and one thing only on her mind.

"Who are the people moving into **MY** house?"

- Chapter Two -

Moving in day

"And here we are," Matthew's dad said welcoming Matthew into their new home. Matthew's dad forced open their new front door. The combined smell of dirt, damp, dust and rot encompassed them. Matthew grimaced, "Lovely."

With one deep breath, Matthew unwillingly stepped foot into his new house. It was even worse than he'd first thought. From the outside the old building looked picturesque, with ivy hugging the crumbling walls.

The inside did mirror the tired look of its exterior. Bare walls with patches of different types of wallpaper revealed several years and tastes of previous occupant's. Woodworms had feasted on the window panes creating holes everywhere. Green mould indulged itself on the hallway carpet and had started to creep into the other rooms.

There was one redeeming feature however, the

spiralling stone staircase. It stretched the depth of the building, strong in character, the back bone of the old vicarage.

"So, what do you think?" his dad asked pacing up and down the hallway with excitement, "gorgeous isn't she?"

'Was he looking at the same house?' Matthew thought.

Not wanting to dampen his dad's enthusiasm Matthew agreed, "Yeah she's really something alright."

"I know it needs a lot of work," his dad said optimistically. Matthew whispered under his breath, "It doesn't need any work, Dad it needs a flipping bulldozer."

"But I think," Matthew's dad continued, "we can definitely put our own 'Khan-McKendry' stamp on the place."

"Yeah, Dad anyway, come on we better start unpacking before it gets dark," Matthew said heading off outside.

Brushing past the withered Willow trees, Matthew meandered along the front path, which took him back towards the driveway.

Approaching the driveway Matthew was startled by a rustling sound from a row of hedges.

"What the?" Matthew said hearing the noise again.

Slowly bending down, Matthew listened more intently. Moving closer and closer he could just about see an outline. There appeared to be an animal hidden within the bushes.

"Oh hello," Matthew spoke gently, not wanting to scare the creature, "You made me jump."

Taking a closer look Matthew could see what had surprised him.

"Oh, hello Mr Crow!"

The crow hopped out from his resting place and joined Matthew on the driveway. The crow looked Matthew up and down, in a curious manner to who was passing by.

Matthew felt nervous as the crow moved closer. Not wanting to alarm the bird he said slowly, "I have just moved in here, well I say moved in we're actually moving in today, me and my dad that is," Matthew stopped himself suddenly realising he was in fact talking to a bird.

Laughing out loud he looked down. "What am I doing talking to a crow? Like **you'd** know what I'm saying."

Unsettled with Matthew's remark, the crow cawed towards Matthew. He wasn't just 'a crow'. He was Clever Crow who had been resident at number 21 for over ten years!

Taken back by the crow's response, Matthew asked, "Did you just caw at me?"

Once again the crow echoed his call.

"Ok now I am losing the plot," Matthew smiled walking towards the removal van. The crow hopped along behind him.

Turning back Matthew asked, "Are you following me now?" Then tilting his head Matthew continued, "can't believe I'm asking this, but what do you want?"

Clever Crow lowered his beak close to the ground. Matthew watched closely and then suddenly he noticed that the bird's foot was bleeding.

"Ah that's what you want," Matthew said, "you want me to help you." Matthew crouched down so he could see what was causing the crow to bleed.

Clever Crow wasn't nervous or scared of Matthew, and trustingly hopped closer towards him.

"Well you are a clever crow, now let me just have a look," Matthew reached down to grab the injured foot, "oh there it is, a tiny splinter of wood, have you been playing too close to some..." And with that Matthew quickly removed the splinter from the crow's bleeding foot.

Clever Crow thanked Matthew in his own way and cawed gratefully for his act of kindness.

Stretching out his silky black wings, the crow

hopped up into the sky. Freely soaring high above the vicarage, he then disappeared off into the distance.

"Come on, Matthew, those boxes won't move themselves!" his dad shouted as he raced past Matthew towards the back of the van.

Looking back at Matthew he asked inquisitively, "What have you been doing out here anyway?"

As Matthew started to help his dad unload, he began to tell him of his encounter with a very clever crow.

After unloading all of their belongings, Matthew began to wander around his new surroundings.

On either side of the hallway were two good sized sitting rooms. Across the back of the house was a farmhouse style kitchen. Cold slabs lay unevenly on the kitchen floor, and piles of dust appeared on every work top. A stable door was hanging crooked on its rotten rusted hinges.

"It just gets better," Matthew commented sarcastically running his fingers along the worktops, creating a plume of dust.

"Let's hope upstairs is better than down here," Matthew said in a rather unconfident tone as he headed upstairs.

"Your room, Matthew," his dad called, "is at the front of the house, just past the bathroom."

"Ok Dad," Matthew gently replied.

Matthew climbed the spiralling staircase and walked along the landing towards his bedroom door.

Gently pushing the door open, Matthew was greeted by the dazzling sunlight which flooded through the doorway.

"Not a bad size and certainly not as dirty as downstairs," Matthew said stepping into his bedroom.

Clever Crow was perched outside his window on a tree branch. Matthew stood against his window and gazed out at the crow.

"Hello again," Matthew smiled.

Suddenly, a knock at the front door disturbed his thoughts. Hearing his dad's voice, Matthew raced along the landing, and to the top of the stairs.

Matthew could just about make out an exchange of words. Wondering who his dad was talking too, Matthew quietly stepped back downstairs.

"We live just across the way, number 23," spoke the stranger.

"I'm sorry, you are?" Matthew's dad asked curiously.

"Oh of course, I'm Pete and this is my wife, Julie."

"Hi," Julie said waving.

"And this," Pete continued, "this is-" but before Pete could finish, Catherine eagerly interrupted.

"I'm Catherine it's very nice to finally meet you mister," Catherine held out her hand as she waited for the response.

Towering above Catherine, Matthew's dad introduced himself, "I'm Mr McKendry, but you may call me Jack. It's very nice to meet you Catherine," he said shaking her hand affectionately.

Noticing that Matthew was now present, Jack turned.

"And this is my son, Matthew."

Catherine was rarely lost for words, but after taking a double look at Matthew, she found herself speechless.

Matthew walked towards her with his hand held out. Just then, Catherine began to giggle nervously.

A little bemused by her funny giggle, Matthew shook Catherine's hand gently.

Matthew's olive skin glowed radiantly in the sunlight. His dark hair was gelled perfectly around his face and his eyes were sky blue. He too towered above Catherine, making her feel tiny.

"It's very nice to meet you, Matthew," she said managing to stop her nervous giggle.

"It's ok," Jack said ruffling Matthew's hair, "lots of girls giggle at our Matty, don't they son."

"Give over," Matthew said pushing Jack's hand away.

Opening the front door wider, Jack kindly invited the three of them in for a drink. Much to Catherine's delight, Pete and Julie accepted.

"Son, why don't you show Catherine around? I'll sort us all some drinks."

Jack, Pete and Julie strolled down the hallway and through into the kitchen.

Coughing to clear her throat Catherine asked, "Your mum, is she moving in later?"

Matthew bowed his head. He didn't feel comfortable talking about his past with a stranger. Without answering her he walked into the sitting room.

Catherine quickly changed the conversation sensing Matthew's unwillingness to talk about his mum.

"How did you find out about this place?" asked Catherine.

"My dad said he saw it on the internet and just put in an offer," Matthew said in a matter of fact manner.

"You're joking," Catherine blurted out.

"I know, but that's **my** dad," Matthew said shrugging his shoulders.

To Matthew's surprise, Catherine spoke passionately of the building.

"Well I think you are really lucky, I love this old

building. I have lived here my whole life and not a single day goes by without me wishing I could live here."

"Why?" Matthew asked sternly, not to sure whether Catherine was being truthful, or sarcastic. "What would anyone see in this dump?"

Catherine didn't respond to Matthew's abrupt question, she was just too overwhelmed to be finally in the place that had captivated her for so long.

Trying to contain her excitement, Catherine went from room to room studying every nook and cranny. Matthew involuntarily followed behind.

"And this is my room," Matthew eventually said nudging the door open, thankful that it was the last room of his tour.

Catherine entered the room and instantly felt the sun light touching the freckles on her face. Looking beyond Matthew's bedroom into the garden, Catherine could see that clever crow!

Overjoyed to see him, Catherine turned to Matthew.

"Have you seen a crow?" Catherine asked.

"Yes I met him earlier," Matthew answered.

"What do you mean you've met?" Catherine said, slightly shocked by Matthew's casual tone about Crow.

With Catherine's full attention, Matthew once

more told the story of his encounter with Clever Crow.

"Well I was going to unload the van when..." Matthew started.

1st May
Dear Diary,

Well it's now 10.30pm.

Mum, Dad and of course me have just come back from visiting the Old Vicarage. Mum didn't want to go across, but thankfully Dad is just as curious as me. The new neighbours are Jack and Matthew. Dad got on so well with Jack that he's invited them to come to the car boot with us tomorrow.

I got to have a good look round. It's not what I imagined it to be, not as mysterious as I always thought it would be. Sure needs a lot of work doing on it. Apparently Jack and Matthew are going to live there, do it up, then sell it on (to me I hope lol.)

Matthew is gorgeous and is only two years older than me. He doesn't talk much, but that will change when he gets to know me. Don't know what's going on with his Mum, maybe she is with someone else, or maybe she's dead.

Oh and you will never believe who is still living there, Crow! Acting like he still owns the place. I couldn't believe he let Matthew touch him. Still at least he's ok.

Anyway early start tomorrow-6am,

Good night.

Oh almost forgot...

Mum and Dad had an almighty fight this morning, Mum accused Dad of having an affair. Dad would never do that.

Also there are NO missing kids hiding in there. Lol

- Chapter Three -

Car Boot mayhem

"Come on Catherine sleepy head, Matthew will be waiting," her dad, Pete, whined at Catherine trying to get her out of bed.

"Oh," Catherine moaned "6 o'clock is too early," she barked.

Pete prowled up and down the landing like a lion hunting its prey, "Come on Cathy!" he roared.

"Ok! Ok! I'm up," finally Catherine yawned.

The thought of spending the day with her new handsome neighbour, Matthew, did make getting out of bed a little easier.

Throwing on her black leggings and her stripy blue-grey jumper, she quickly noted,

2nd May
Dear Diary,

Just a quick note as it is 6.15 in the morning! Setting off to the

22

car boot soon for the first time in ages, I can't wait. I get to spend the whole day with Matthew. Wait till I tell everyone at school, they will be so jealous, especially Abigail.

Bye for now xxxx

Catherine placed the diary in her colourful fabric bag.

"Hair brushed, check, teeth cleaned, check, best clothes on, well we are going to a car boot, leggings and jumper will do, looking good? Check." With that, she threw her bag across her shoulder and skipped happily downstairs.

Pete, Julie, Jack and Matthew were stood waiting for her.

"Hi everyone," Catherine said trying to sound lively.

"Hi Catherine," Jack replied. Matthew just nodded his head.

"Come on then there's no time to waste if we want to get all of the good stuff," Pete said, grabbing his car keys off the sideboard.

Pete, Jack and Julie lead the way to the car while Matthew and Catherine dragged their feet along behind.

"What's in the bag?" Matthew asked.

"Oh it's just my diary she, I mean it, comes everywhere with me."

"Hum," Matthew mumbled.

"So, have you been to any car boots before?" Catherine asked Matthew, trying to spark a conversation.

"Nope," Matthew replied rather abruptly as they both got into the car.

It wasn't too long until Pete announced they had arrived.

"Right, Jack let's leave these young ones to fend for themselves," Pete put his arm around Jack's skeleton shoulders. Julie headed off in the opposite direction leaving Matthew and Catherine alone.

Hardly a blade of grass could be seen underfoot. Stalls were tightly packed together in the shape of a horseshoe. Crowds of people swarmed around the stalls, like bees after honey, creating a vibrant atmosphere.

Catherine turned to Matthew, "Come on, shall we have a look around? You never know, we might find something of interest."

"What here?" Matthew said sarcastically.

"Come on," Catherine smiled urging Matthew on.

"Ok," Matthew said softening towards Catherine, "you'd better show me what's what then."

As they began to walk around the horseshoe field, Catherine explained how it had become a ritual to come here every Sunday. Some families attended Church, some visited garden centres, others rested but for Pete, Julie, and Catherine the car boot had become their family outing.

As the day went on, Matthew started to feel more comfortable with Catherine. Matthew told Catherine about the times he and his dad would play football. He told her about how they stayed up on Saturdays to watch match of the day. Catherine didn't follow football, but she enjoyed listening to Matthew talk.

Meandering through the stalls they observed all sorts of weird and wonderful things that were for sale. Something's were quite nice, but many things were just people's unwanted stuff.

"Well I think you're right, Catherine," spoke Matthew.

"Right about what?" Catherine asked curiously.

"About it being a waste of time," Matthew laughed.

"Not as boring as football though," Catherine fired back smiling.

"Hey!" Matthew replied pushing Catherine softly.

Catherine blushed and lowered her head. Looking back up at him, Catherine realised Matthew was looking past her.

Set back from the other stalls, through the swarm

of people, sat a little old man scrunched over on a stool. At first glance, Catherine and Matthew couldn't quite make out what he was selling, but found themselves intrigued by the attention he was getting. They started making their way through the crowds to get a closer look.

Edging closer, Catherine turned to Matthew, "I think he's selling sweets."

"Let's hope so," Matthew grinned rubbing his hands together.

As Matthew and Catherine approached the stall, the crowds parted allowing them through. The old man looked up at them both and Catherine and Matthew smiled nervously back at him.

The old man ruffled his long grey scraggy hair. He tried to straighten his crumpled long black coat which was keeping his frail body warm and hidden.

"Hello," the old man murmured wearily.

"Hello," Matthew replied. Catherine just about managed a smile.

Grabbing Matthew's arm Catherine whispered, "He seems a little strange let's go back."

"No chance, I'm going to get us some sweets," Matthew said brushing Catherine's arm away.

Looking down at the colourful jars, what at first had appeared to be sweets, were in fact tiny bugs all cramped together scurrying around searching for food.

Gasping in shock, Catherine squeezed Matthew's arm again.

"Please let's go," she pleaded.

Matthew and Catherine turned and started to walk away from the old man.

"Oh please don't go," the man spoke calmly whilst rising to his feet, "I'm sorry if the bugs scared you they're for my bird you see, she loves them!"

The old man reached down to retrieve something from under his table.

"Wow," enthused Catherine, "she's beautiful."

The old man placed down in front of them, a silver steel birdcage. Inside was a brilliant white dove, which sat perfectly still.

Catherine moved back towards the stall and stretched out her hand to touch the cage.

"Don't touch her!" the old man ordered, causing Catherine to jump back.

Realising he had startled Catherine the old man calmly added, "I'm sorry, my dear, it's just she gets very nervous around new people. It's probably best to leave her alone."

Then turning his attention towards Matthew, the old man lowered his voice, "I think you, my boy, might like this."

Reaching beneath his table once more, he slowly unveiled a snow globe.

"Wow, it's amazing," Matthew said completely mesmerised by the object.

Catherine couldn't quite believe Matthew was being serious. It was the ugliest snow globe she had ever seen. It had a black metal base, and the only thing occupying the glass dome was what appeared to be a castle. Instead of glitter, black dust occupied the globe. To Catherine it seemed nothing special.

Seeing how interested Matthew was in this piece of old junk, Catherine felt compelled to speak up.

"Matthew, are you being serious? Look at it!" Catherine picked up the globe and started to shake it, "It's rubbish! Look even the snow is black. Come on!"

"Snow?" the old man addressed Catherine crossly, "why would there be snow?"

"Because that's what snow globes have, hence the name 'snow' globe."

Catherine was starting to become annoyed with the old man's attitude. She thumped the snow globe back on the table and urged Matthew once more to walk away.

But Matthew had become more and more curious with the object. Reaching out to touch the globe, the dove began to flap its wings uncontrollably and pecked viciously at the bars trying to break free. The dove's squawk pierced Catherine's ears as it became more and more frantic. Matthew watched on unaffected by the dove's antics.

"Silentium, Silentium!!" the old man shouted aggressively towards the dove.

Following the old man's instructions, the dove retreated back on her perch.

"Now, Matthew, where were we?" The creepy old man sent shivers down Catherine's spine. She felt the air go cold, and as the wind picked up she desperately wanted to leave.

But the old man continued, "You're Matthew Khan, aren't you?"

"How do you know my name?" Matthew demanded, shocked by the old man's question.

"Matthew, I think we should go and find our parents," Catherine pleaded again.

Darkness began to descend as the birds of the air climbed steadily into the thunderous clouds which gathered above. Catherine pleaded one more time for Matthew to hurry along, but her words were silenced by the roars of thunder.

"How do you know my name?" Matthew shouted, trying to make himself heard.

A flash of lightning followed before the old man

leaned forward towards Matthew and whispered "Because I knew your mother."

Matthew jumped back in shock, "My Mother!? You knew my Mother?" Matthew's olive skin turned pale. No one had spoken of his Mother's whereabouts for years.

Regaining Matthew's full attention the old man went on to explain, "She gave me this for you and told me one day you would find me."

The old man raised the snow globe to give to Matthew, however, his actions once more caused the dove much distress.

The dove circled her cage like a raging bull ready for a fight, knowing the dark secrets hidden within the globe. Volunteering to take the snow globe, Matthew cupped both of his hands together and waited for the old man to deliver.

Happy to depart from it, the old man placed the globe into the palm of Matthew's hands. Then the old man let out a belt of laughter to which the skies above responded. Deafening thunder resounded around the now empty field.

Matthew stood solid, his eyes fixated on the globe as the old man's laughter changed into an evil chortle.

Catherine had heard that sound before. Closing her eyes she focused her attention on that laugh, that chuckle, that evil chortle.....that caw?

Catherine, now wide eyed, shook her head in disbelief. How could it be?

As Matthew clasped the snow globe, the black dust came to life and started to swirl around the castle. Responding to Matthew's touch the globe glowed brighter.

Matthew could feel the snow globe becoming warmer, and the palms of his hands turned deep red. The globe stuck to Matthew's hand as though magnetised, and its power intensified the more Matthew resisted its pull.

Completely paralysed by its power, Matthew could see the tiny little castle inside the globe beginning to melt under the intense heat. Hotter and brighter the globe shone, until the light reached high into the clouds above.

Again the thunder roared and Catherine quickly turned to Matthew, "Drop it Matthew!" she ordered.

"I can't!" Matthew shouted back.

Fear filled his eyes and as the light became more powerful, the old man lifted high above them.

"You fool!" he bellowed down to them.

The old man's body rose high above them. The light from the globe formed around him. His grey hair started turning as black as the night, his dirty muddy coat cleaned itself of any dirt. The old man's withered, wrinkled, gaunt face began to shrivel up.

Catherine and Matthew watched on in astonishment as the screwed up face formed into a sharp, sleek beak.

His weary aging eyes transformed in shape and colour, shrinking smaller and smaller until they were two jet black beady eyes.

The transformation was complete as the old man finally revealed himself. Stretching out his fine wings, he gave an almighty caw and swirled high above Matthew and Catherine.

Now soaring above them, he peered down to see them standing helplessly below. Catherine and Matthew gazed on in awe as he danced with the lightning which flashed brilliant white against his majestic black. Another sequence of caws echoed throughout the field.

The heat of the globe had begun to crack the glass, and with one almighty clash of thunder it shattered into a million pieces. The castle had completely liquefied and began spilling out onto the mud. The heavy clouds opened up their arms allowing water to fall down from the skies.

Matthew, now finally free of the globes power, ran over to embrace Catherine.

Feeling his arms around her Catherine turned to face him, but his eyes were watching Clever Crow.

For Clever Crow was now soaring high above them ordering the heavens when, and when not to speak. Clever Crow who Matthew had helped on his driveway was now thanking Matthew in his own very special way.

Catherine, tear filled and shaken turned to Matthew, "What have you done? What have you done?"

- Chapter Four -

Darkmoor begins

Matthew and Catherine stood shocked and stunned by what they had just witnessed. Furthermore, they realised that the crowds of people had somehow vanished. The ground below had become waterlogged. Catherine began to sob as she tried to make sense of her surroundings. She closed her eyes praying to wake up any minute, but as Catherine dared to open them again, Crow's shadow lured overhead.

"Look, Catherine, look there," Matthew said pointing down towards the mud.

A spark of light flickered in front of them, then another and another.

"Look, Catherine, did you see that?" Matthew asked.

Catherine wiped her tears off her cheek and looked down.

The castle which had previously flooded out of the broken globe had created a puddle of mercury. Its thick silvery creamy texture glistened as lightning struck all around. Droplets of water fizzed violently as they fell into the pool of mercury.

"Oh my," Matthew said grabbing Catherine, "Look!"

As they stood in astonishment, the mercury fused itself with the rain and little silver veins started to flow out into the darkness. Suddenly, the earth started to rumble beneath their feet causing Matthew and Catherine to fall down into the mud. Their eyes widened and their bodies trembled. A mighty rumbling sound shot up through them and into the sky above.

"Quick move, Catherine!" Matthew called out as the land cracked around them.

Realising that they might fall into the void, they quickly scrambled to their feet. After slipping several times in the wet mud, they managed to get away from the danger. Finally, the earth quake stopped and there in front of them was a continuous void which weaved itself from East to West.

Catherine grabbed Matthew's arm, "You're going to be ok Catherine, I promise," he said.

From within the cracks of the ground came a piercing, deafening sound which caused Matthew and Catherine to cover their ears. Looking back towards the void, Matthew and Catherine's eyes widened in amazement.

Suddenly, out of the empty void shot a black arrow which was twisting and turning through the air. Its sharp, sleek beak cut cleanly through the night. With his wings pulled down by his side, Clever Crow continued to spiral through the heavy clouds like a tornado. Climbing higher and higher, majestically he silhouetted against the bright moon. Then Crow emitted a final screech.

Crow stopped abruptly, unfolded his wings and started to flap them quickly trying to catch the wind. Hovering above Catherine and Matthew, Crow's beady eyes darted across the land below. Firmly focussed on Matthew and Catherine suddenly, Crow tucked his wings back down at his side.

"Get down!" Matthew shouted pulling Catherine down into the mud.

Crow thundered down towards them, accompanied by another bout of screeches. Crow whooshed past them, his dagger claws narrowly shaving their hair. Flying only a few inches from the ground, Crow turned back around and aimed once more for the two youngsters.

However, this time Matthew stood tall with his feet pressed firmly into the mud. Matthew raised his hand up to hit out at Crow, who attacked him with his razor sharp claws.

"Ouch!" Matthew screamed.

Catherine, still with her head in her hands, frantically asked, "Matthew! Matthew! Are you ok?"

"Yeah I'm fine. Where is he? I think he's gone!"

Matthew looked down at the back of his hand. Crow's razor sharp beak had slashed it open, causing ruby red blood to pour out and down his fingers.

"Matthew," Catherine said noticing Matthew's blood, "you're hurt!"

"It's only a little cut, I'll be fine," Matthew said smiled through gritted teeth. Throbbing pains shot up his arm and Matthew felt his cold blood pulsating faster.

"Where is he?" panicked Matthew looking up towards the sky.

"I don't know."

Silver mercury started to jet out from the cracked walls, filling up the void before them. Within in a few minutes, the once empty space was full of silver liquid, which soon illuminated the dark sky. Calmly the silver, creamy, river flowed gently lapping against the river banks. Up from the river bed silver veins sprouted and slithered across to the opposite side. Churning deep into the mud, the sparkly veins of mercury awoke the buried trees. Creaking for joy the trees happily welcomed the blood of life, pushing past the life sucking mud and stretching their baron branches towards the rays of the moonlight.

Gazing across the opposite side of the river, Matthew and Catherine witnessed the slithers of mercury performing their healing touch upon the woodlands.

Directly across from them, on the other side of the river, a familiar figure rustled out from within the trees. Silently, Crow stared back towards them.

Gaining their full attention, Crow slowly submerged his whole body into the river and sank gently down to the river bed. Catherine and Matthew could just about make out Crow's motionless shadow. Then once more Crow opened his mighty wings and started to flap them furiously, causing silver droplets to rise into the air creating an enormous silver cloud.

Completely mesmerised, Catherine and Matthew stood speechless as every little drop of mercury vacated the void, leaving it dry. Crow stood masterful in the now enormous empty space, and dragging his wings back, fired himself back up into the dark sky.

Using his sharp black beak, Crow cut open the cloud causing white mist to snow down and fill the empty void. Crow then darted down once more and plunged himself head first into the newly created misty river.

Catherine and Matthew could feel their hearts pounding in fear, but couldn't stop watching, waiting for Crow to return. But Crow had vanished and had been replaced by a human figure, which began to stroll across the bottom of the void.

Catherine and Matthew watched on nervously. The 'thing' trudged itself along, leaving slivers of silver mercury on its well worn boots. As the mist lifted, both Matthew and Catherine were able to observe the figure's thick black hair cascading down his back. Brushing his hair back, the figure tilted his head skywards and roared an evil laugh.

"Who is he?" Catherine said trembling with fear.

Matthew's throat was bone dry, leaving him unable to speak.

Hearing Catherine's voice, the dark figure quickly turned. His long black hair swished around his long narrow face. Casting his burning eyes onto Catherine and Matthew he called across,

"There's no need to whisper Catherine, I have the hearing of a crow don't you know!"

"Did you eat him? Did he eat him?" Catherine screamed back at him in disgust then looked towards Matthew for some reassurance.

Matthew just shrugged his shoulders, and the man started to laugh again.

"Oh my dear," the man said sarcastically sympathising, "I am Crow." His mocking laughter shook the ground. Trying to make sense of what had just happened, Catherine fainted into the mud.

Matthew looked down at her, feeling unable to help.

"How can that be possible?" Matthew asked nervously.

"If I told you that Matthew, then I would have to kill you!" the man stared hard towards him.

"How do you know who I am? And what is this place? And you who are you?" Matthew asked quickly.

The man paused for a moment then answered, "Well it's a very long story Matthew, one which I will share with you some day, but for now I have some work to do."

"Wait…" Matthew called anxiously towards the man. "How could you be?"

"Oh it's very easy if you know how. Being the crow and then the old man, I thought would be the easiest part, but tricking you, well that was just too easy!" the man once more laughed mockingly across at Matthew.

"But who are you now!?" Matthew asked sternly.

The man's eyes narrowed and Matthew felt vulnerable as he stood there alone. As the man's mood seemed to darken, the atmosphere grew cold around them. The rain clouds rumbled and the lightning crashed down around him.

"Silentium! Silentium!" the man shouted up towards the sky, causing the heavens to silence.

Whispering he teased, "Just three simple words, Matthew, that's all."

"What!" Matthew shouted back.

"I am," the man opened up his arms and looking up to the sky continued, **"I am Darkmoor!"**

Thunder and lightning accompanied his announcement, making the earth shake. As the explosive thunder echoed through the land, the trees started to sway. The storm roared on as Darkmoor turned his back on Matthew.

The tremendous sound made Catherine awake from her coma and shaking her head, she tried to make some sense of her surroundings. Noticing Matthew standing on the river side, Catherine managed to scramble to her feet.

Noticing Catherine standing besides him, he grabbed her hand tight.

Sensing they were still watching him, Darkmoor knelt down in the wet dirt. Placing his fingers into the mud he circled them around creating mud pies at his feet. Lifting his dirty hands into the sky, Darkmoor clapped them twice. The thunder and the lightning obeyed Darkmoor's command.

"Awake! Awake! Advoco! Advoco!" Darkmoor called as he stood over his mud pies. Suspending his hands over the mini mountains, Darkmoor spoke again.

"Advoco!" Instantly summoning the monsters buried in the mud to arise.

Recognising their master's voice, one by one they reformed themselves from the tiny mud mounds to mighty monsters.

As mud dripped off the monsters bodies, Catherine and Matthew could truly appreciate Darkmoor's masterful magic.

Each monster was covered in black shabby hair, except for two hairless arms which protruded out from under their manes. Their arms formed down into three fingers which swished about like elastic dangling in the dirt. No legs were needed as the monsters skimmed across the mud.

They had long and narrow jaws like wolves, with saliva drooling uncontrollably from the corners of their crooked snouts. Opening their mouths they revealed razor sharp white teeth. Suddenly, they started to howl for their master. Big, dark, fearsome eyes bulged out of their sockets, which darted around as they sniffed the cold night air.

Matthew stood there both fascinated by Darkmoor and scared by what Darkmoor was doing. As he lined up his troops one by one on the river side opposite them, Darkmoor called across in a chilling voice.

"Matthew, I look forward to seeing you again soon!"

"Please Sir," Matthew pleaded, "How do we get home?"

Darkmoor chuckled loosely causing his troops to howl, "Do you really think I would tell you that? Ah poor Matthew and his little friend trapped in Darkmoor. Where would all the fun be if I let you go home? And besides, you two should know I am the master of **all** tricks!"

And with that, Darkmoor turned his back on Catherine and Matthew and retreated through the dense woodlands. Clapping his hand twice the monsters stood to attention, and then like soldiers they followed their sergeant into the darkness.

Then, Darkmoor and his mighty monsters were gone.

- Chapter Five -

A light in the darkness

Catherine scurried around in the mud, frantically searching for her bag.

"It has to be here somewhere, Matthew," she panicked, digging in the mud.

"What?" Matthew asked.

"My bag and diary, I'm sure, wait, never mind I've found it!"

A relieved Catherine quickly pulled open her bag to check if her diary was still inside. With a pen in one hand and the diary in the other, Catherine leaned over the blank pages ready to write.

"What date is it today, Matthew?" Catherine asked in a confused manner.

"Are you crazy!?" Matthew asked, astonished at Catherine's relaxed attitude, "haven't you realised what's just happened to us?"

Here they were lost without anything, or anyone. The car boot sale had completely vanished, the comforting sound from the swarms of people had faded long ago, and yet here Catherine was acting as if nothing had happened.

Looking up at a bewildered Matthew, she shrugged her shoulders, "What?"

"You seriously think now is a good time to be writing in your precious diary!?"

"I have to! I write in it every day. It will only take a few minutes and besides there's nothing else to do!" Catherine lifted the diary up close to her face. Steadying it on her knees she started to write...

Dear anyone,

Help us, please if anyone can read this, please help we're trapped in,

"Where are we, Matthew?"

A place called Darkmoor, or is that the man's name. The man is Crow!! It's all very confusing, but once I know more I will let you know. It's dark, wet, cold, and we are both really scared. So please if you find this help us.
Yours hopefully,
Catherine Rose and Matthew Khan.

Catherine ripped the entry from her diary before

placing it back into her bag. Then standing up, she threw the bag over her shoulder.

"What are you going to do with that?" Matthew quizzed Catherine.

"I am going to find somewhere to leave it and hope someone will find it." Catherine answered as her eyes searched her surroundings.

"You really think someone else is going to come here?" Matthew asked sarcastically.

"Yes I do," Catherine replied trying to sound positive.

As Catherine looked at Mathew she felt saddened. He stood with his head hanging down towards the floor, twirling the mud round with the tip of his trainer. She stepped closer to him and put her hand gently on his shoulders, then said, "Matthew, look at me. We have to believe we are not the only ones here." Catherine paused as Matthew lifted his eyes up from the ground to meet Catherine's gaze.

But Matthew's eyes appeared hard and cold towards her. A sense of dejection was written all over his face.

"Look around us, Catherine. Do you really think anyone else would live here?" Matthew spoke sternly.

Removing her hand off his shoulders, Catherine stepped back as she felt her eyes fill with tears.

The wind gradually blew stronger. The sound of bare tree branches chattered together and the ground underfoot was like a mud bath. As the silence descended around them both, Matthew reached out for Catherine's hand.

"I'm sorry Catherine, it's not your fault." His eyes softened and he smiled at her.

"Come on," he continued, "we can't stay here, let's try and find some shelter."

Together they walked along the river bank, their feet squelching in the mud.

"This is **so** horrible," Catherine whined as the mud started crawling over her white pumps, then camouflaging itself against her black leggings.

"I know," Matthew replied looking down at his soggy clothes.

They walked along the river for what felt like miles. Their bodies shivered uncontrollably in the cold air. The moon shone through the broken trees casting ghostly shadows upon the ground. Fearfully, Matthew and Catherine shifted their eyes from left to right as they continued deep into the unknown.

"I really hate this, Matthew," Catherine shivered as she clung tightly onto his hand.

As the moonlight moved across the ground a tiny light flashed, then faded. Catching Matthew and

Catherine's attention, they waited for another flash to appear.

Eventually, as the moon hovered over the ground, again the tiny light glistened out. This time it seemed more powerful, coaxing Matthew and Catherine to investigate.

Moving nervously closer, the white light flashed on and off.

Twinkling in the moonlight, laying flat down on top of the mud, was a silver hoop. It sparkled like jewellery and Catherine's eyes widened with curiosity as Matthew reached down to retrieve it.

Suddenly, realising what Matthew was about to do, Catherine shouted "Stop!"

"What!" Matthew replied standing to attention.

"Have you forgotten what happened the last time you held something?" Catherine said sarcastically. "I'll pick it up," Catherine smiled as she brushed past him. Then, taking a deep breath she carefully wrapped her fingers around the object.

"Hum," she frowned, "it appears to be stuck! I think we'll have to dig it free."

Without hesitation, Matthew put his hands into the mud, "Well, come on!"

Kneeling down in the moist mud they started to dig. Bits of soggy mud spat up into their faces.

As they continued, they began to uncover some metal bars which extended out from the silver hoop. Finally, freeing the whole object from the mud, Catherine and Matthew could now truly appreciate their hidden treasure.

"Wow!" They admired.

Lying sideways across the ground was the silver bird cage Catherine had admired earlier at the car boot sale, and sitting perfectly still on her perch, was the dove.

Her brilliant white coat, despite her muddy surroundings, was spotless and warming. Looking up to inspect her rescuers, the dove immediately recognised the two youngsters and softly cooed graciously towards them.

Matthew carefully lifted the cage out of the mud and held it up. Dove's glorious white light cascaded like a waterfall down from her head and out of her feathers. It fell gracefully around her delicate toes and stretched out to cover, Catherine and Matthew.

Placing the cage gently back on the ground, the dove hopped off her perch and pushed her delicate beak along the metal bars. Anxiously, Matthew turned the tiny silver door knob and placed his hand into the cage.

While Catherine held her breath, (remembering the last bird that she and Matthew had helped), the dove brushed her soft, silk feathers along Matthew's hand.

"Come on it's ok. I won't hurt you," Matthew spoke softly, reassuring the bird.

Trustingly, the dove stepped into Matthew's muddy hand. Slowly he took his hand out of the silver cage and lowered her to the ground.

Free from Matthew's grip, she opened up her pure white wings. They sparkled with the light of the moon and lifting herself up into the dark sky, the dove took to the air.

Dancing in the strips of moonlight, her beautiful wings twinkled like fairy dust. Awakened by the dove's presence, tiny stars scattered across the sky line. An overwhelming feeling of comfort filled Matthew and Catherine, as together they watched her silhouette gracing the night sky.

Finally, the dove hovered above Matthew and Catherine. Sprinkling what appeared to be fairy dust upon them both, she guided them along the muddy paths. They followed trustingly behind her, hoping she was leading them to shelter, or better still, home.

Suddenly, from out of the darkness, sounded a didgeridoo. It caused the ground to shudder.

"What is that?" Catherine asked as her eyes bulged.

"I don't know," Matthew replied.

Just then, flaming arrows shot over the woodlands and started to set alight the dark sky.

The dove started to flap her wings faster and the two youngsters jogged on behind her.

Leading them off the river side and through a break in the trees, the bird began to coo. Another low tone rumbled and a dozen more fiery arrows blazed overhead.

"It's ok, I can see them, they're with Dove."

"Seize fire!"

Pushing their way through the broken branches, Matthew and Catherine finally managed to follow the dove deeper into the woodlands. Dove began to flap rapidly forcing herself up high into the sky, until eventually she was out of sight.

Feeling completely alone, Matthew and Catherine tiptoed further into the forest. It wasn't long before they discovered the true reason the dove had brought them into the forest.

Towering high into the sky were two thick wooden gates, held in place by two solid pillars which stood tall like candlesticks. Dazzling, fiery bright amber light flickered out from the tops of the pillars.

"Oh my," Matthew gasped.

"What the," Catherine stuttered.

Stepping closer, Catherine noticed something was

engraved in the withered wooden gates. Nervously, Catherine placed her finger onto the etchings. At first she flinched and pulled her hand back, but then regaining her original stance, Catherine once again placed her fingers back into the carved out wood.

Twirling them around, she spelt out the letters in her head.

"What is it, Catherine?" Matthew asked.

"There's writing on the gate," Catherine answered pointing towards it, offering Matthew to read it for himself.

Intriguingly, Matthew started to slither his fingers across the slimy, moist surface, before sounding out the words.

"The forgotten"

"What do you think that means?" Matthew asked Catherine, wiping the slimy goo on his jeans.

But just then, the heavy wooden gates started to creak. Taking a step back Catherine whispered, "I think we're going to find out."

As the doors began to open, a burning light filtered out through the narrow gap and an aroma of burning logs surrounded them. Matthew and Catherine basked in the heat of the fiery warmth. The didgeridoo rumbled once more and finally the gates opened wide.

Orange, red and yellow flames climbed up into the night sky, accompanied by the sound of the wood cracking under the fires intense heat. Together they walked towards the giant camp fire, and anxiously entered the land of 'The forgotten.'

- Chapter Six -

The Forgotten – Part 1

The heavy wooden gates slammed shut. A shadow emerged from the smoke of the fire, and excitedly trotted towards them.

"Hi, you made it," said the young man who was approaching them.

Matthew and Catherine stood there bewildered as the young man continued, "I'm Nathan and you are?" he asked trying to engage them into conversation.

"Oh sorry, I'm Catherine and this is Matthew."

"Well we're all glad you're here, follow me," Nathan smiled.

Nathan's sandy blonde hair rested upon his shoulders. A thick wavy beard came to a point off the end of his chin, and his piercing blue eyes smiled comfortingly towards Matthew and Catherine.

Surrounding the fire was a carpet of mud, and piles of wood were scattered around. Five circular shelters surrounded the camp fire in a horseshoe shape, and each one appeared to be hand made out of hardened mud. Individual wooden doors and small gaps had been created to allow some light in. Broken tree branches entwined together sat on top of the mud huts, acting as roofs. Raindrops dripped down from the roofs and formed puddles, which ran around the huts like moats.

High upon the perimeter wall, which encapsulated the camp, sat three human figures. All three were armed with bows and flaming arrows, apparently guarding the 'forgotten.'

"There are ten of us here now," Nathan commented in a matter of fact manner. Nathan continued by rhyming their names off, "Andrew, Claire, Jasmine, and not forgetting our most recent, Thomas and Isabella..."

"Wait, who?" Catherine asked interrupting Nathan.

Nathan slowly repeated, "Thomas and Isabella. They arrived about-"

"Two weeks ago," Catherine said quickly finishing Nathan's sentence.

Catherine stared into the fire. She watched the flames dancing to the tune of the wood crackling. Her legs turned to jelly causing her to fall down onto her knees. Placing her head into her hands, Catherine wept.

Shrugging his shoulders, Matthew turned to a bewildered Nathan.

"How do you know that?" Nathan asked Catherine calmly kneeling down next to her.

"Because, I know them," Catherine sobbed.

Nathan stood up, scratching his overgrown beard he turned and walked towards the muddy shelters.

"Please," Matthew spoke grabbing Nathan's arm, "please tell us what this place is and how we can get home?"

Turning back to face Matthew, Nathan's eyes softened, placing his hand upon Matthew's shoulders he said, "I will, I promise, but first I have to tell the others you're here."

With that, Nathan walked off into the mud huts reassuring the others that it was safe to come out. One by one the camper's emerged, reluctantly at first, but eventually they made their way towards the two new arrivals.

Nathan looked up towards the three soldiers and shouted, "Olli! Claude! Reuben! Come down and meet our latest recruits!"

Upon hearing Nathan's orders, the three soldiers' gave him the thumbs up in unison. Dipping their flaming arrows into buckets of water, they began making their way down towards the centre of the camp.

Matthew helped Catherine up from the dirt. She had just about managed to stop herself from crying, when out of the first mud hut two small children charged towards her.

"Cathy! Cathy is that you?"

"Cathy! Cathy!"

Immediately Catherine recognised those tiny voices. Opening her arms wide she called back, "Thomas, Isabella!"

Rushing into Catherine's open arms, Isabella and Thomas giggled with glee. Catherine's eyes filled with tears of joy.

"It's so good to see you both, how did you end up here?" Catherine asked pulling herself away from their warm hug.

"Come and sit next to the fire," Isabella said holding Catherine's hand. Pulling her closer to the roaring fire, Matthew followed. Catherine and Matthew sat down on a couple of tree stumps which circled the fire.

"Well everyone, this is Matthew and Catherine," Nathan introduced them and a bunch of strangers smiled sympathetically towards them.

"Hi," they said in return, shyly waving their hands.

Nathan asked every one to take to their stumps, "Ok, so you already know Isabella and Thomas."

"Get off Nath Nath," Isabella chuckled as Nathan squeezed her chubby rosy red cheeks. Isabella had beautiful golden curls which flopped wildly around her face and as her big brown eyes looked up towards Nathan, he couldn't resist bending down and hugging her. Isabella chuckled even more, which soon became an infectious laugh around the camp.

"Oh you are a cutie Issy busy!" Nathan gave her a final squeeze then, as he walked past Thomas, ruffled his hair which caused Matthew to reminisce.

"It's ok" Dad said as he ruffled his fingers through my hair, "lots of girls giggle at our Matty, don't they son!"

"Give over Dad!" I said shoving my Dad's hand away...

"Matthew! Matthew! Are you ok?" Catherine's faded voice brought Matthew round from his daydream.

"Yeah, yeah I'm fine," Matthew whispered as he brought his attention back to Nathan.

Thomas grinned. Placing his tongue between the gap, where two front teeth were missing, Thomas wiggled his tongue towards Nathan.

"Oh you cheeky monkey, I'll have that Tommy tongue next time," Nathan said snipping his fingers like pincers towards Thomas.

Next to Thomas was another young man, probably in his late twenties.

"Hi I'm Andrew," Andrew stood up and walked

over to shake Matthew and Catherine's hand. Then he returned to sit back on his stump.

Next to Andrew was Claire and Jasmine. Nathan smoothly kissed the back of their hands whilst introducing them.

"Oh Nathan! Get off," Jasmine said wiping the back of her hand down her pants.

Claire didn't seem to mind his affection. Her eyes lit up to his tender touch. Winking towards her, Nathan then carried on around the circle.

The three soldiers had now taken to their stumps.

"And these three," Nathan said as he pointed towards the three African boys, "are Olli, Claude and Reuben."

"Hi I'm Reuben," the oldest of the three said and lent over to greet Matthew and Catherine, "this is my brother, Olli-"

"Hi," Olli said and waved towards them.

"And this is my other brother, Claude."

"Hi," Matthew and Catherine said in unison.

Catherine asked, "Are you triplets?"

"No!" Claude said abruptly.

"Oh I'm sorry, it's just you all look so alike."

"It's ok, Catherine," Reuben said, "I am the oldest, then Claude, then our Olli."

Catherine couldn't help but stare at their amazing

hair styles. They all had the biggest Afros she had ever seen.

"Our hair wasn't like this when we arrived," Reuben commented.

"I didn't mean to stare," Catherine quickly spoke.

"Ha, don't worry about it. Being in here you forget about looking good and of course, there are no hairdressers!" Reuben smiled at Catherine.

"Right then, I think that's everyone," Nathan said.

At that moment, a booming knock at the wooden doors silenced them all. The fire flickered frantically as the atmosphere chilled around the camp.

Crash, boom, bang, the sound once more echoed throughout.

"Darkmoor," Matthew whispered under his breath. Matthew's heart began thumping hard, as the knocking became more persistent.

Matthew could feel himself becoming increasingly agitated. Catherine fixed her eyes upon him and both Nathan and Andrew gave the order for Jasmine and Claire to take everyone into their shelters.

"Quickly, to the shelters now," Jasmine said calmly, not wanting to frighten Isabella and Thomas, who were innocently watching everyone rushing around. Catherine picked Thomas up and Claude quickly scooped Isabella up into his arms.

"Matthew! Matthew! Come on!" Catherine called down to Matthew, who was transfixed with the dancing flames of the fire.

Darkmoor's eyes burnt into mine, as across the white misty river, we faced each other. His deep grinding voice shouted, "Matthew! Catherine! I look forward to seeing you both again soon!"

"Matthew…"Jasmine crouched down at his side. Placing her arms around his shoulders, she softly spoke, "Look at me, Matthew."

Vacantly, Matthew looked up into Jasmine's eyes.

"Come on, come with me," Jasmine said gently easing Matthew to his feet.

"It's me he wants, Jasmine," Matthew blurted out.

Jasmine quizzed "Who?"

"Darkmoor!"

Just saying his name drained Matthew's body of colour and energy. His eyes rolled back in his head and his heavy body flopped lifelessly into Jasmine's arms.

"No!" Jasmine called, "Reuben help!!"

Chapter Seven

The Forgotten – Part 2

Together, Reuben and Jasmine carried Matthew's limp body into one of the shelters. Placing him slowly onto the floor, Reuben whispered, "Poor kid."

"I know," agreed Jasmine, "but you know Reuben, he spoke of Darkmoor."

"So," Reuben murmured as he stood peering through the tiny gaps.

"So, how does he know about him?" Jasmine asked.

"I don't know," shrugged Reuben.

"Look," Jasmine started, "when we arrived here we didn't know where we were, or who Darkmoor was, right?"

"Right," Reuben said in agreement.

"So...."Jasmine held her arms open, anxiously waiting for Reuben to answer. "Come on Reuben!" Jasmine shouted impatiently, "how does he know!?"

Reuben looked sharply at Jasmine, "You think he's actually met Darkmoor?"

Clapping sarcastically Jasmine grinned, "Yes, finally, flipping heck Reuben."

"Alright," Reuben accepted, with a somewhat vacant look.

Squatting down in a separate mud hut, Catherine and Claude clung tightly to Thomas and Isabella. Catherine didn't know what to say, without Matthew she felt vulnerable and alone.

"So, you and Matthew," Claude started, "are you brother and sister?"

"No, we hardly know each other," Catherine smiled nervously, "we are sort of, well you know."

"Friends?" Claude asked.

"Yeah I suppose so," Catherine swallowed hard. "You see he moved in across the road and I had to go and see, even though my Mum didn't want me too, but the crow. Well I had to know if he was ok," Catherine paused for breath, not making sense as she spoke, "and anyway here we are."

Claude shuffled closer to Catherine. Isabella was fast asleep in Claude's arms, Thomas tried his hardest to stay awake, but finally gave into temptation.

Claude gently placed Isabella into one of the handmade beds. Each one consisting of green vines interwoven together and tree stumps were used to elevate the beds up, out of the mud. Isabella opened her eyes as Claude covered her little body with a smelly old blanket.

"Goodnight little cutie," Claude whispered gently.

"Goodnight Claude," Isabella responded in her angelic voice.

Then bending down, Claude kissed her forehead. Isabella closed her eyes once more and fell fast asleep.

"Here, give me Thomas," Claude whispered taking Thomas' sleepy body from Catherine. Thomas flopped effortlessly into Claude's arms, then just had he had done with Isabella, Claude covered Thomas' sleeping body. Catherine smiled.

Suddenly, Nathan's voiced echoed throughout the mud huts, "It's ok, it's only Sam."

"Who's Sam?" Catherine asked Claude.

"She's in charge."

"Oh," Catherine said puzzled, "I thought Nathan was."

"Yeah, that's what Nathan thinks too!" Claude laughed as he strolled back out towards the fire.

Everyone huddled around Sam, but Catherine stayed well back. The sound of chattering filtered up through the night sky.

"So, where are the new comers?" Sam's Scottish voice boomed.

Catherine watched and waited for Matthew to step forward, but nothing.

The crowd in front of Catherine parted, as she walked uneasily through the camp towards Sam.

"I'm here Miss," Catherine bowed her head. 'Where was Matthew?' she thought.

"You must be Catherine?" Sam asked.

Slowly Catherine lifted her head. Standing straight in front of her was a small stocky woman, whose hair was braided and pulled back from her face allowing her emerald eyes to shine.

Handing her bow and arrow to Nathan, Sam introduced herself, "I'm Sam, you didn't come alone did you, Catherine?"

"No," Catherine stuttered, "I came with Matthew."

"Hum," said Sam moving away from Catherine, "well, where is he?"

Sam stared past Catherine, noticing that a young man was standing in the doorway of the hut. Catherine quickly turned her head, glad that Matthew was at last present.

Stepping past Catherine, Sam headed towards Matthew.

Placing her arm across his shoulder she whispered, "So, Matthew, Jasmine tells me you have met Darkmoor?"

Matthew looked into Sam's eyes. A shiver shot down his spine as she mentioned Darkmoor's name. Opening his mouth to speak, his throat became dry.

"Listen to me, Matthew," Sam's soft voice turned stern, "I don't want anymore talk of Darkmoor, we will talk afterwards, just me and you, is that clear?" Sam's word's sounded more like an ordered than a request. Unsure of what to say, Matthew said nothing, and giving Sam a crooked grin, he followed her down to the camp fire.

Perching himself next to Catherine, Matthew asked, "Are you ok?"

"I am now, what did Sam want with you?" Catherine lowered her voice, not wanting Sam, or the others to hear her.

"She just said she wanted to talk to me after supper that's all," Matthew replied casually, not wanting to unnerve Catherine.

"She just wants to talk to you, what about me? We did come together."

"I don't know, maybe she wants to speak to us both. She mentioned Darkmoor and then got all funny about it."

"That's weird, well actually, all of this is weird. What do you think is going to happen to us?"

"I don't know," Matthew said meeting Catherine's gaze, "but somehow, we will get home."

Catherine looked down, not wanting Matthew to see the disbelief in her eyes.

"Catherine, Catherine, it's me that got us here and I swear to you, I will get us home." Matthew spoke certainly, gripping Catherine's hands and squeezing them tight.

"Hey you two," Sam shouted across the camp, "Matthew! Catherine! You two ever had wolf-lizard before?"

"A what?" Catherine asked lifting her head up to look across at Sam.

"It's one of the many creatures here, not one you would like to come across daily, but they do taste pretty good!" Sam explained as she held up one of the monsters. Sam had been out of camp hunting for food, and had somehow managed to capture one of Darkmoor's mighty monsters, using only her bow and arrow.

"A perfect shot, straight through the heart, killed it instantly," Sam boasted. "You see, only a bow and arrow will do," Sam went on, "with their tongues of fire tightly rolled in their snouts, ready to whip out at any moment. Then, with one fatal strike, you would be dead!" Sam bluntly explained.

Whilst Sam had been educating everyone, Nathan and Andrew had been skinning the beast. Sam began to skewer her hairless catch ready to spit roast. The wolf-lizard's long arms limped down into the pit of burning ash, leaving no part of the creature uncooked. Sizzling, popping and cracking accompanied the aroma of burning skin throughout the camp.

"Well, that's supper sorted," Sam said proudly.

Everyone began to sit back round the fire. Sam sat opposite Matthew and Catherine.

Nervously, Catherine asked her, "So, how long have you all been here, Sam?"

"I've been here for twelve years, Nathan, Andrew, Claire and Jasmine arrived about eight years ago. The three Afro boys arrived next, then the two wee ones, and now you." Sam waved her hand as the smoke thickened around her.

Not being able to remain quiet, Matthew asked shyly, "And this, this is Darkmoor?"

Sam looked crossly at Matthew and a deafening silence descended around the camp. A cold draught blew up from the ground causing the flames of the fire to flicker rapidly.

Matthew could feel Sam's eyes burning through him, but feeling an overwhelming confidence welling up inside of him, more assertively he asked again, "And this is Darkmoor?"

"How do you know that, Matthew? How do you know his name?" Sam questioned him.

The atmosphere intensified between Sam and

Matthew, as everyone else remained still and quiet.

"Well!" Sam shouted, prompting Matthew to reveal all.

"Because," Matthew started, "because he told me." The other campers gasped in amazement at Matthew's revelation of speaking to Darkmoor.

Sam leaned closer towards him, "Carry on," she insisted.

Gathering his thoughts, Matthew paused for a moment, then with everyone's full attention, he began to tell of his experience.

"Well, it all started when I moved into the Old Vicarage opposite Catherine, and there lived a crow, but only he wasn't a crow..."

Upon telling his and Catherine's story, Sam silently stood to her feet. Using a twig she poked the beast, clear juices oozed out of the well cooked creature and dripped on the fire, causing it to spit and hiss.

"Right everyone it's supper time," Sam announced causing everyone to race off to clean up ready for dinner.

"Not you, Matthew and Catherine, we need to talk!"

Leading them towards one of the huts, Sam closed the rickety door behind them and sat down upon a camp bed.

"Look you two, I have been here for years and apart from me, no one else has ever seen Darkmoor, no one." Sam lowered her voice as she mentioned his name, "I don't want you to cause any upset, it's bad enough without you two stirring things up. Do you hear me?"

"But I don't understand, what do you mean, no one else has met him? Who is he Sam? What does he want with us?" Matthew's voice was full of desperation.

"Look, Matthew," Sam started her voice softening, "he's your worst nightmare. He doesn't care how, or what he kills, it's his way, or no way. I don't know how or why we are here, but somehow we are. Look, I know you would love to get home, all of us would, but you have to realise that we are-"

"What Sam? We're the forgotten?" Matthew voice rose as he interrupted her, "Sam, I have to go and find him, I have to understand why, I can't live here forever!"

"Matthew, I will not have anyone, and I mean anyone, go over there! Do you here me!" Sam ordered, "this conversation is over!" And with that Sam stood and turned to walk away.

"No!" Matthew called to her, "no Sam it's not! I will meet Darkmoor again and I will get home!"

Turning slowly back to face Matthew, Sam's eyes narrowed. Matthew walked over and whispered in her ear, "You can either help me or not, but I will not be forgotten, I would rather be killed than spend the rest of my life in here. Do **you** hear me?"

Matthew looked sternly at Sam as he stepped away from her. Without saying anything else, Sam smirked before turning her back once more and returned to the camp fire.

Turning to Catherine, Matthew grabbed her arm tightly causing Catherine to motion backwards, "I will take care of you, I mean you're mine."

"Get off me!" gasped Catherine, "what are you doing?"

Catherine shuddered, as an unrecognisable Matthew stood before her. His eyes were pure black as they pierced Catherine's eyes. His olive skin was now burning red with anger. Catherine silently left the mud hut.

Standing alone in the darkened shelter, Matthew couldn't get Darkmoor out of his head. The back of his hand started to throb, and the more Matthew remembered the day's events, the more his body drained. Laying himself down on one of the beds, Matthew closed his eyes tightly.

Darkmoor is marching out of the mist. He is facing me now, and I can feel his dark piercing eyes burning through my skin and searching my soul. His long black hair is swaying in the chilling breeze and then, suddenly, he commands his wolf-lizard's to kill me.

"No, please no!" I am shouting, but there is no one to hear me. I am alone.

The deadly monsters are plunging themselves one by one into the white misty river and have started to wade across. I can see their fiery tongues whipping around their sharp white teeth.

My legs are numb, my whole body is shaking.

Where is Catherine? Just then, I remember Catherine, my Catherine.

His laughter starts to roar out across the land followed by screaming, Catherine. I hear her screaming, calling for me, Catherine!

I can't get to her, Darkmoor has her.

Silence is descending around me. All the while his mighty monsters are coming closer. I look across the river to see Darkmoor. He is taking her away into the darkness. Then, I can't see anymore, the darkness has swallowed them up and Catherine has gone.

"No, Catherine!!" I shout, but she can't hear me calling.

"Catherine!"

- Chapter Eight -

Reuben's Story

Soaked in sweat, Matthew opened his eyes and wiped the sweat off his brow. Still breathing heavily from his living nightmare, Matthew's eyes darted around the room before focusing upon the grey sky, which peered through the gaps in the roof. Matthew removed his dusty torn blanket and made his way outside.

Sat next to the camp fire, trying to reignite it was, Reuben.

"Morning Reuben," Matthew spoke gently as he approached him.

"Morning Matthew, did you sleep at all?" Reuben asked as he threw some more twigs onto the fire.

"Yeah I actually dreamt of-" then remembering Sam's warning, Matthew quickly changed the conversation. "So you and your brothers, have you been here long?"

"Yeah about six years I guess, you sort of lose track of time in here." Reuben replied staring into the fire.

Watching the dancing flames steadily grow, Reuben couldn't help but think back to the day that changed his life forever.

"*Reuben! Reuben! Where are you?*" *Mama's strong African accent boomed throughout the house, causing the pictures hanging on the walls to rattle.*

"*Reuben!*"

"*Mama I am here!*" *I shouted back from the kitchen. Her feet thundered down the hallway in my direction.*

"*Don't raise your voice to me young boy!*" *Mama said waggling her finger. There was no reasoning with Mama, you were best saying nothing at all except,* "*Sorry Mama!*"

She stood wobbling from side to side in the kitchen doorway. Her big hooped earrings swayed frantically as she glanced over the tops of her rectangular glasses.

"*Yes, Mama?*" *I asked nervously, trying to think of what I was in trouble for this time!*

"*I'm going to the shops, so I need you to watch Claude and Oliver for me.*"

Oh great, Claude was stubborn and never did anything without objecting first. And Olli, well he was Mama's little angel, or so he led her to believe, but every time she left me in charge, he would always get up to mischief.

Through my fake smile, I reluctantly agreed.

Mama stomped back up the hallway bellowing up the stairs to Claude and Olli, "*Be good!*" *(Yeah right, I thought)* then slamming the front door behind her, she was gone.

Upon hearing the door close, Olli immediately came charging downstairs and into the kitchen.

"What we gonna do, Reuben?" Olli eagerly asked.

I sighed. I couldn't be bothered to do anything. Olli asked again, only this time his eyes grew wider with excitement. Coupled with a cheeky grin, I couldn't resist his enthusiastic and persistent request.

Bending down to pick him up in my arms, I asked stupidly, "What would you like to do, Olli?"

"Play football?"

Of course! That's all Olli ever wanted to do, play football. At the age of six Olli lived and breathed the sport.

Begrudgingly I said, "Ok, better tell Claude."

Whilst Olli ran off to get his football from under the stairs, I shouted up to Claude. With no reply, I shouted up again, "Come on Claude, Olli wants to play football!"

Dragging his feet across the landing, I could hear Claude muttering under his breath, probably cursing me, but I didn't ask.

"Right, we all need our coats on it's cold out there," I ordered, trying my hardest not to sound like the nagging older brother (or mother come to think of it!)

"If it's cold, why don't we just stay in?" Claude stated.

"Because, Olli wants to play out and I can't leave you here alone," I replied calmly.

"We always do what Olli wants, it's not fair," Claude complained, but nevertheless continued fastening up his duffle coat.

I didn't reply, I couldn't be bothered to argue with him. Helping Olli fasten his buttons, I then grabbed my coat and the three of us trudged off into the cold winter air.

Frost nipped at our fingers and toes, it was freezing. The snow filled clouds hovered overhead, I was certain it would snow any minute.

Claude stood at the road side, his arms firmly crossed. This time I couldn't really blame him for sulking, as the cold air had already started to numb my body.

Olli didn't seem to feel the frosty nip though, he ran up and down the street with his football.

"Olli!" I shouted. "Don't go near that old building!"

"Ok Reuben!" Olli's voice echoed down the road.

I rubbed my hands together trying to warm them up. Claude was almost blue, his teeth chattering together like a woodpecker against wood.

"Reuben, please I'm freezing, can we go back in now?" Claude pleaded.

I didn't argue.

"Olli, come on!" I called taking a few steps towards home.

"Olli, come on, it's freezing!" I shouted louder. Still there was no answer.

Both Claude and I shouted, but nothing, not even the sound of his football bouncing. Just silence.

Frantically gazing onwards, we both ran up the street desperately searching as we made our way towards the run down vicarage.

That place sent a shiver down my spine. It stood alone at the end of our street, a rumbling wreck which could tumble down at any minute. Mama had severely warned us to stay away.

Edging closer towards it again I shouted, "Oliver!"

Tiptoeing up to the boundary of the Old Vicarage, my heart thumped against my chest.

Peering over the wall, our eyes quickly darted back and forth through the broken windows.

Sitting still upon the doorstep, minding his own business, was a crow. Although more importantly, we had found Olli and relief came over me. I smiled and called towards him, "Come on you cheeky thing."

Without warning, Olli set off running up the garden path towards the crow. Before I knew it, Olli had disappeared once more.

This time he had run into the old building, that old vicarage, followed bizarrely by the crow.

"Quick!" I commanded, "run! We have to get in there and get Olli!" thankfully Claude didn't need telling twice.

Together we raced around the broken wall, across the cracked driveway and headed straight through the open doorway.

"Olli, where are you?" I whispered, not wanting to waken the nasty ghosts Mama had warned us about.

"Olli, Olli," Claude whispered.

"Boo!" Olli jumped out scaring us both, causing us to jump back and accidently forcing the front door to slam shut.

I tried to open it, without success. I yanked harder, but couldn't force it open. It was as though, somehow, it had locked itself.

"That's weird," I said quietly to myself, not wanting to frighten Claude or Olli.

"We will have to find another way out," I said passively.

Holding my brother's hands, we slowly crept down the hallway of the derelict building. The floor boards creaked as we continued our way through the eerie soulless place. A cold chill shot down my spine and I became more and more uneasy about being there.

Olli glanced up at me, his eyes flooding with tears, his bottom lip trembling and an overall sense of fear written all over his face.

"I'm sorry Reuben, I just wanted to stroke the crow," Olli began explaining with tears tickling down his face. I couldn't get mad, he didn't understand.

"Listen Olli, I will get us out of here, don't worry." I didn't even believe what I was saying, but Olli wiped his eyes and nodded confidently.

"Look there's a light on down there," Claude pointed

towards the staircase which disappeared into the cellar below.

"I'm not to sure that's a good idea, Claude," I don't know why but something inside was telling me to run, run as far away from that place as possible.

But Claude being Claude, convinced me he knew best so, I let him lead us down the wooden steps and into the dusty, damp cellar.

It was empty, nothing. A light blub was spinning round as it freely dangled from the ceiling. The sound of bugs and insects echoed through the hollow space.

"I don't like this," I felt nervous, but Claude and Olli had already reached the bottom step.

Once I joined them, I realised the cellar wasn't completely empty. Sat under the staircase was the crow which Olli had chased, and positioned next to the crow, was a snow globe.

"Come on let's not scare the crow," I said turning to walk back up the wood wormed riddled stairs.

Olli could resist though. I should have grabbed him there and then, I should have played the mean big brother card, but regretfully I didn't.

I let him run over to the crow. I let him pick up the snow globe. I watched in slow motion as the crow flapped his wings in temper. I watched as Olli dropped the globe causing it to smash into a thousand pieces on the floor. A cold icy wind blasted throughout the room, growing stronger and stronger.

The howling wind engulfed our screams as an unstoppable force dragged us towards the broken glass.

I reached out to grab Olli and Claude, with all my might I pulled them into me and told them to close their eyes. The hurricane like wind reached its maximum intensity, causing the light blub to shatter. Then darkness!

Cautiously I opened my eyes. We were no longer in the damp, cold, cellar and we were no longer in the cold winter air.

Everything had vanished. Our feet became wetter, darkness enveloped us. I looked down at the ground. Mud had replaced the hard cellar floor. We were outside, but not on our street. Claude and Olli clung on to me, not wanting to look.

That crow, the same crow as before, was soaring high above us and up into the heavy stormy clouds. He cawed down at us in temper. Then, he just disappeared.

"And then?" Matthew asked sitting on the edge of his stump, lingering on Reuben's every word.

"And then," Reuben repeated staring into the incessant fire.

"And then somehow, we ended up here," Reuben swallowed hard trying to keep his tears at bay.

Matthew stayed quiet for a moment before asking, "The vicarage, Reuben, where was it?"

But before Reuben had chance to answer, Sam's

shadow appeared over the two of them, and quickly Reuben turned.

"I was just telling Matthew," Reuben's voice shook nervously.

"I know what you were telling him, Reuben!" Sam said crossly causing Reuben to stand and cowardly retreat back to his hut.

Sitting down on Reuben's warm stump, Sam looked intently at Matthew. "Now then," she started, "I think we should talk about last night, don't you?"

- Chapter Nine -

Preparing for Darkmoor

Dear Diary,

You will never believe this, but Matthew and I are not alone. Yesterday we found a place called the forgotten, whatever that means! Anyway Thomas and Isabella are here along with lots of other people.

Sam is the lady in charge. She and Matthew are talking by the camp fire as I write.

The camp is ok. They have built mud huts for houses, which are very cold! And beds made out of trees, not quite luxury, but better than a muddy floor!

I'm still not sure what has happened to us. I don't know if we will ever get home, although Matthew promises me we will. I really miss Mum and Dad.

Catherine momentarily stopped writing. Tears fell onto the page, and she tried to find the words to express her feelings.

Anyway, I don't really feel like writing much more. It makes me sad. I'm going to talk to Matthew.

As Catherine wrote the words she could hear Matthew shouting, then Sam crossly instructing him to calm down. Quickly flinging her diary across the bed, she raced towards Matthew.

Matthew was stubbornly looking at Sam, and Sam was sternly looking back at him.

Walking around the back of Matthew, Catherine stroked her hand gently across his tense shoulders, but Matthew didn't respond. Sitting herself beside him she asked, "Is everything ok?"

Sam coughed, Matthew snorted, and Catherine didn't dare asking again.

From the corner of her eye, Catherine clocked Nathan approaching them. Carrying a pile of freshly cut logs, Nathan asked, "Hi guys, how are tricks?"

Catherine shrugged her shoulders. Nathan looked at Sam then at Matthew before playfully jabbing Sam.

"Well, Sam," he went on to say, "I think you've met your match."

Quickly shifting her eyes from Matthew to Nathan, Sam sighed, "Weren't you suppose to be getting breakfast sorted, Nathan? I suggest you do!"

Nathan nodded his head and rapidly walked away to collect some more fire wood.

"You are not going, Matthew!" Sam stated with intent.

If looks could kill, Matthew would have dropped dead right there.

Not intimidated by Sam, Matthew rose to his feet. Stepping closer and towering over Sam, he replied assertively, "I am going, so you can either help me or not, but I will cross the river and enter Darkmoor."

Sam dismissed Matthew and turned towards Catherine, "What are you going to do then… Catherine?"

Catching her off guard, Catherine stuttered, "I… I…"

"Go on," Sam demanded, "are you going to follow your boyfriend?" she added sarcastically.

Matthew took a few paces away from camp, his head bowed as he blushed about what Sam had said.

Watching Matthew walk away from her, Catherine suddenly stood to her feet and called after him, "I'm coming with you!"

Turning back to face her, Matthew's smile widened, "What?" he asked.

Lifting her arms up into the gloomy grey sky she said, "How could I not? I mean, well, erm."

Matthew continued to smile at her and Catherine could feel her cheeks burning red. Letting herself get lost in his eyes, she almost forgot where she was.

"Hum," Sam coughed breaking Matthew and Catherine's gaze, "You two are crazy, but,"

Matthew darted his eyes across to Sam, "But...?" Matthew asked rapidly.

"But if you're so determined to get yourselves killed, then I suppose I shouldn't stand in your way," Sam flashed a crooked grin at Matthew.

Trudging towards him she patted his shoulders, "Don't be too thrilled, Matthew, I'm coming with you!" Accompanying Sam's promise was a roar of laughter which explosively echoed throughout camp.

Dear Diary,

Me, Matthew and Sam are going to cross that white misty river tomorrow. I couldn't let him go without me. Anyway, we are practising how to use a bow and arrow after breakfast. Apparently that's the only way to kill Darkmoor's monsters. I can't believe this is happening to me. I always thought adventures of mysterious lands where just make believe, and here I am trapped in one. I really hope I don't die, I'm too young to die! Please God if you're listening, please keep us safe, please!

I wonder if there is a poster of me and Matthew missing?

Right, that's Claire shouting everyone to wash up before breakfast so bye for now.

Catherine closed her diary and hugged it tightly. All her memories were stored between those pink leather covers. Everything she ever thought about, everything she'd ever done, even happy times with Crow. Catherine shuddered as she thought of him, that big black crow who had watched her for years. Scared of what they might find across the river, somehow despite her fears, Catherine felt ready to face Crow or Darkmoor, whoever he, or it, was.

★ ★ ★

"Right Catherine, Claire is going to show you how to fire arrows, and Andrew is going to show Matthew," Sam spoke with authority.

"And you?"Matthew asked, "what are you going to be doing?"

Sam smiled as she picked up her own bow and arrows, "Me, Matthew? There's something I need to collect." Sam's voice faded as she walked away towards the heavy wooden gates, guarding the entrance, "I won't be long, good luck!" she shouted back waving her hand towards Claude and Reuben. Receiving their orders, the two boys heaved those wooden gates open, allowing Sam to disappear into the distant darkness.

Matthew turned to ask Andrew, "What did she mean? Something to collect?"

"I'm not to sure," Andrew continued, "she doesn't really explain a lot, but don't worry she'll be fine," he said smiling nervously at Matthew.

Mesmerised by those gates, longing to disappear beyond them, Matthew felt his hand starting to throb. The more Matthew thought of Darkmoor, the more the pain increased. Feeling his body draining of energy as the pulsating throb continued, Matthew just about heard Andrew calling from across camp, "Matthew, are you coming? Come on!"

"Yeah!" Matthew called looking down at his wounded hand, "I'm coming!"

Matthew and Catherine spent all afternoon learning how to use their bow and arrows. Catherine picked it up almost immediately (much to Matthew's annoyance) but after a lot of determination, eventually Matthew managed to pick it up too.

"So, don't forget, you only fire at them if you really need to, one clear shot will kill a wolf-lizard immediately," instructed Andrew.

"Have you ever killed one?" Catherine asked turning to Claire and Andrew.

They both looked at each other, "No thank goodness, but you two, well you know," Claire replied, biting her lip.

"What Claire is trying to say," Andrew continued

for her, "you will have Sam with you so you'll be fine!"

"Yeah, we'll be alright, I think?" Matthew muttered.

Archery class was soon over, Sam returned back to camp, and was once more accompanied by a dead rancid wolf-lizard.

Night time descended, once again everyone gathered around the camp fire. No one spoke for ages (not even Nathan), an awkward atmosphere grew as they thoughtfully watched the flames flicker.

"How did you get on today, Matthew?" Reuben asked breaking the silence.

Lifting his head, Matthew realised everyone (including Sam) was waiting for him to answer. Coughing to clear his throat, Matthew muttered out, "Good thanks, Reuben."

"Cathy," a delicate little voice spoke. Isabella's beautiful smile lit up the whole camp, looking innocently at Catherine, Isabella continued, "When you see my mummy and daddy, will you tell them me and Tom are ok, they will be really worried about us you know, won't they?"

A lump formed in Catherine's throat, opening her arms she invited Isabella up onto her knee. Hugging her tightly, Catherine whispered, "I promise."

Matthew watched as Catherine brushed her fingers

through Isabella's curls. Sensing a cold icy stare coming from across the camp, Matthew lifted his eyes to meet Sam's stare through the smoky fire.

"What did you go out of camp for, Sam?" Matthew asked.

"This," Sam remarked in a matter of fact tone, as she held up a telescope.

Taking her eyes off Isabella, Catherine looked up, "What is it?"

Sam walked towards Matthew and Catherine and held it out for them to have a closer look.

"It's a telescope," Matthew said sarcastically before taking it off Sam.

Putting his eye over the lens of the telescope, almost immediately an expression of astonishment swept across his face.

"Wow," Matthew gasped, "camp looks so bright, I mean, wow!"

At first glance it appeared to be a normal telescope, having one large and one smaller glass lens at either end. The lens was fixed firmly in place by a brown leather bind. It looked like a piece of average kit, but was clearly different to a 'normal' telescope.

Again, Matthew took another look through the lens and again the camp shone bright, as if the sun was overhead.

Popping Isabella onto the empty stump next to her, Catherine grabbed the telescope to take a look for herself. She pulled the object quickly away from her eye, then quickly back again.

"Wow!" she too exclaimed.

"How? I mean what is it? How is it doing that?" asked a very puzzled, but intrigued Matthew.

Realising that she had the camper's full attention, Sam started to explain, "Well, it's what I call a light catcher. It makes the night appear like day, it's that simple. In Darkmoor it's always night, it's just the way he likes it, but with this," Sam said taking the light catcher very carefully off Catherine, "we'll be able to see which way to go and of course, if there's any danger heading our way!"

Sam then went onto explain how delicate it was and how she had hidden it out of camp for safe keeping. Gently she placed it back into her rucksack.

"Right you two," Sam said addressing Matthew and Catherine, "we set off early in the morning so try and get some rest, believe me, you will need it."

Picking up her belongings, Sam took herself off to bed leaving Matthew and Catherine to say their goodbyes to the other campers.

Dear Diary,

I am trying to sleep, but I can't. I am so scared about tomorrow, I wish we were home.

I feel like crying when I think of what we are doing, but I can't back out now, he needs me. We practised using a bow and arrow today. I'm pretty good at it, but Matthew struggled picking it up! Anyway, we now have a bow and arrow ready to use just in case. I really hope I don't have to use mine. I don't like the idea of killing things.

My eye lids are starting to feel heavy, so hopefully I will get some sleep. I wonder if Matthew is asleep.

Well, goodnight xxxxx

- Chapter Ten -

River of Souls

I'm standing here alone. I have to cross, the monsters are coming. It's my only way to save Catherine.

My foot steps automatically onto the first plank of wood. The bridge begins to sway from side to side. The wolf-lizards are getting louder and louder, I can sense their stale breath on my cheeks.

I'm not going to look at them, I have to focus on the bridge. My body is shaking, my legs are trembling and something is pulling me across.

I lift my head to look, there she is, Catherine. She's reaching out her hand for me to take. I reach out my arms stretching to touch hers, for I know just one touch of her hand and we will be free.

"Catherine, Catherine!" I call, but suddenly he's there instead.

Darkmoor.

He's laughing at me, suddenly I lose balance. I start to sway on the rope bridge, the monsters begin nipping at my ankles, then snapping, then really hurting.

"Help!" I scream. "Help!"

My hand is throbbing the pain is becoming too much. I can't do this, I...

"Matthew, Matthew," Catherine called shaking Matthew.

His olive skin had turned white as snow, tears of sweat flowed down his fear-filled face, gasping for breath, Matthew's body trembled.

"Are you ok? You seemed in a world of your own," hearing Catherine's voice again, slowly Matthew turned his head.

Brushing his hands through his hair, Matthew managed to calm himself down before smiling back at Catherine, "I'm fine," he said remembering his daydream before continuing, "listen, Catherine I don't think it's a good idea for you to come with us, it's not safe."

"Well I am!" Catherine snapped at him.

"I don't want you to get hurt," Matthew started as Catherine crossed her arms, impatiently waiting for an explanation. Chuckling to himself Matthew conceded, "Never mind, I'm not going to win am I?"

"No you're flipping not!" Catherine replied flashing a warming smile at him.

"Well we have to cross it! The river of souls, that's if you still want to go and see Darkmoor?" Sam's voice interrupted, "or are you having second thoughts?" she continued sarcastically.

Lingering for a moment, Matthew looked intently into Catherine's eyes. He felt like it was the first time he'd really looked at her. Catherine's hazel eyes smiled affectionately towards him, her red hair hung loosely around her face. Overwhelmed with a sense of protection, Matthew muttered under his breath, "Oh Catherine."

Matthew turned and stared across the white misty lagoon and the rickety rope bridge draped across it.

"I'm ready!" Matthew said confidently.

With their bows and arrows securely fixed across their backs, Sam, Matthew and Catherine cautiously stepped onto the wooden bridge. Matthew muttered under his breath, "Well, this is it!"

Leading the way was Sam, followed by Matthew and a very loaded up Catherine nervously trudged behind. Her bag was strapped around her waist, her weaponry fastened across her back. Matthew couldn't help chuckling to himself as she reminded him of the game, Buckaroo!

"Be careful!" Sam shouted back to Matthew and Catherine, "some of the wooden slats are rotten!"

Catherine tiptoed behind Matthew copying his every move. Blisters formed on the palms of her hands as she clung tightly to the ropes, but blocking out the pain she steadily proceeded. Underneath them the white mist started to churn.

Sam boomed, "Don't look down!"

"The river of souls?" Catherine asked, "why is it called that?"

Not hearing Catherine clearly, Sam repeated her words, "I said, don't look down!"

The bridge began to creak as a gentle breeze blew across. As they continued further along, the wind grew fiercer and cautiously they took one step at a time.

Matthew's heart pounded and thumped, the palms of his hands gathered sweat. Obeying Sam's instruction not to look down, Matthew fixed his eyes firmly on the other side of the river.

Suddenly, out of the swirling mist erupted a myriad of screams, shrieking and wailing. Despite the deafening, ear-piercing noises, Catherine couldn't help but look down.

Underneath her, floating on top of the river, were four ghostly angels dressed in full length white gowns. Their faces were pure white with long transparent hair floating ruggedly around their tiny heads. The four of them looked up at Catherine, who found herself hypnotised by their graceful angelic smiles. Catherine watched on as the angels performed, like synchronised swimmers diving in and out of the mist. Free of the mist, they arched their backs and gracefully drifted gently back into the river. The painful screeching noises had now stopped, however, the white mist had begun to slowly creep over Catherine's feet, encircling her.

Catherine's eyes grew wider with both excitement and anticipation.

'They're so beautiful,' Catherine thought, feeling her hands release from the rope, she knelt down on the wooden bridge.

Moments later, one of the angels emerged from the mist. The angel grabbed a startled Catherine's hand and began to forcefully drag Catherine down towards the river.

Opening her mouth wide, the angel's face began to change. Her pure angelic eyes turned to a burnt red like fire, her teeth sharpened like daggers, her transparent hair turned as black as night. Then, from between her lips, out darted a lizard like tongue. Jolting her head back, the angel snapped and whipped her bloody tongue around her mouth, stroking her razor sharp teeth. She screamed at the other three angels, who instantly appeared behind her.

Upon her command, each angel took hold of Catherine. A strange tingling sensation came over Catherine, particularly in her face. Under some sort of spell, Catherine found herself not wanting to fight their persistent power rather, Catherine was happy to embrace them.

"Catherine! Catherine!"

Catherine lifted her emotionally drained head up towards the thinning fog. In slow motion, a tall dark figure emerged out the mist. His eyes widened as they focussed upon her. His mouth was moving, but she couldn't hear any words.

Catherine snapped aggressively at the stranger as he made his way closer towards her.

The angels turned to face the intruder, with a snap of their heads their fiery tongues lashed out. However, this intruder was determined. Ignoring their warnings, he kept firmly focused on Catherine.

Looking up at him, a spellbound Catherine studied the fearless figure. Confusion cast over her face, as something deep within her battled against the evil which had hold of her.

Leaning down, his soft warm hand stroked her cheek, "Get off me!" Catherine snarled, pushing his hand away. Her voice sounded deep and deadly, but the stranger didn't give in.

Their eyes met, Catherine's face began to change back to its original form, then suddenly evil.

"It's me," spoke the boy's voice once more.

Catherine's face began to shift back.

Keeping calm, the voice persisted, "It's me, Matthew. I've come to save you!"

Pulling her hands away from the angels, Catherine reached up to touch his face. Catherine's face returned to its normal state, revealing a warm smile.

"Come on," Matthew calmly spoke, picking up Catherine's weak body.

The angels shrieked with anger as they plummeted. Matthew lifted Catherine's lifeless body into his arms, and started to walk towards the banking. However, their moves were followed promptly by the angels, who swam like sharks in an attempt to block the exit.

The angels gnashed their teeth aggressively, so much so that blood began to pour out of their scolding eyes. Lizard like tongues slapped furiously against the wooden bridge in temper, causing it to sway uncontrollably.

Cackling like witches, they flew towards him. Before he had chance to react, they had surrounded him. Gripping Catherine's lifeless body tight, Matthew closed his eyes.

An almighty thunderous sound echoed throughout the land.

"Amitto! Amitto!"

"Darkmoor?" Matthew remarked out loud, clinging tightly onto Catherine.

Immediately, the ghostly angels descended back into the mist. The atmosphere became calm as Matthew opened his eyes slowly, he realised, with some confusion, that standing over him, was Sam

"I thought you were-" Matthew began before Sam interrupted him.

"Never mind all of that, they won't stay down there forever, we need to move fast!"

Matthew didn't need ordering twice and quickly he ran straight for the river bank, carrying Catherine to safety in his arms.

Finally free from the ghostly angels, Matthew slowly placed Catherine's limb body onto the muddy floor. Realising that Sam hadn't followed him, Matthew looked back across the bridge.

Sam was still there. The ghostly angels had remerged and were hovering over her.

Their faces had reformed back to their delicate angelic state, and Matthew watched intriguingly as the angels seemed to respond to Sam.

Just then, Sam lifted her hands up into the air, and once more called out,

"Amitto!"

Upon hearing her words, the angels gracefully descended back into the river and, instantly, the white mist became still and silent once again.

Puzzled by Sam's authority over the angels, he looked down towards Catherine as she approached.

"She'll be fine," Sam said flippantly.

"Yeah I hope so, Sam," Matthew smiled, then looking up at Sam he asked, "What did you just do?"

"Just do?" Sam answered sounding a little confused.

"With the angels, you made them go back into the river."

Sam darted her eyes back across the now calm river, "Oh you know..." she stopped and paused, before continuing, "You just have to speak like Darkmoor and then they obey."

The fallen silence was broken by a murmuring Catherine. Her eyes flickering open then shut. Rubbing her hands across her forehead, she asked "What happened? My head is killing!"

"You passed out, again!" Matthew said sarcastically, holding out his hand to help her up.

"Passed out, what do you mean?" puzzled Catherine. "But my mouth hurts, my eyes, oh my eyes feel like they're bleeding!"

"Well," Matthew started, "we had to cross the river and you..."

- Chapter Eleven -

Where wolf-lizards tread

"We'd better move, we don't want to be out here when night falls," Sam murmured as she rummaged through her rucksack, revealing the light catcher.

Grey sky grew heavy, ice cold air crept slowly around them and they sensed that the night was fast approaching.

Sam peered through the light catcher at what seemed an endless vast forest.

Offering the light catcher to Matthew, he nervously positioned his eye over the lens.

At first he jumped back and his hands started to tremble. Tiny beads of sweat gathered on his forehead, but intrigued nevertheless, he took another look.

'How could such a dark, dangerous, deadly place be transformed into one of beauty, one you longed to step foot in, one you would be happy to explore?' Matthew thought whilst peering one more time into Darkmoor's land.

"I can't get over it, how does it, you know?" Matthew said reaching out his hand, trying to grab hold of the rays of sunlight, desperately longing to feel the warmth of a normal summer's day upon his skin.

"Ok, ok," Sam intervened clasping hold of the catcher, "like I said, we'd better move!" Returning the light catcher into her rucksack, Sam started to walk along the path and into the suffocating darkness.

Catherine remained quiet, with one swift smile towards Matthew she marched quickly behind Sam. Slowly but surely they edged towards the forest, leaving behind the river of souls. Matthew quickly gathered his belongs and he too followed on behind Sam.

"Are you ok back there?" Sam asked.

"Yeah thanks," Matthew shouted back, his voice echoed through the forest.

Overhead the branches appeared to be woven together, acting like a canopy.

"Oh get off me, get it off!" Catherine screamed throwing her bags onto the path as she started to jump around.

Sam quickly got her bow and arrow ready to fire.

"What? What is it?" Matthew asked keeping his distance.

"It's, it's a spider!!" Catherine shouted flicking at her clothes.

Matthew couldn't help but burst into laughter, Sam smiled too, "Matthew don't just stand there, help me!!" Catherine shouted.

"Oh come here, Catherine," Sam said strolling up to her and flicking the bug onto the floor, "there it's gone!"

"Are you sure, I can still feel it crawling on me."

"That will just be the beetles!" Sam said teasingly.

"Ha ha very funny, glad your amused," Catherine said sarcastically.

"I'm sorry it's just that..." Matthew began then stopped.

"What, it's just what?!" Catherine said putting her hands on her hips.

"It was only a spider! Sure you're not scared of the evil swimming angel looking vampires, but spiders, that's when you really freak out!" Matthew said jokingly.

"Ok, ok I can't help it, they give me the creeps!" Catherine bent down to pick up her belongings. "And anyway, everyone is scared of something!"

"Yeah monsters, aliens, wolf-lizards, that sort of thing," Matthew said teasingly.

Catherine gave him a killer look, "You think you're so funny..."

"Ok you two, should we get on?" Sam interrupted.

Both of them nodded their heads, and once again the three of them set off through the forest.

Night had fallen and a cold icy breeze blew gently through the woods, causing the broken tree branches to clumsily clatter together. Tiny insects scurried around underfoot searching for their next feast. Catherine couldn't help shuddering as she could feel the tiny creatures crawling all over her. Not wanting to make another fool of herself in front of Matthew, she bit her lip tightly and screamed in her head. Matthew's head bowed down towards the floor, lost in his own thoughts, wondering whether he would ever see home again.

At that moment an almighty gush of wind howled throughout the forest and the lifeless trees creaked violently.

Then at the edge of the forest, encircling them rapidly, like a lion hunting its prey, that all too familiar fog formed.

"Nobody make a move," Sam ordered with her arms wide apart shielding Matthew and Catherine.

"Why? What is it? What's going on?" Catherine whispered, darting her eyes between Sam and Matthew.

Slithering like a snake across the ground, the life form fog rapidly closed in on its prey. Gliding over the barren forest, the fog breathed its breath upon the trees causing them to stretch their limbering branches. The hungry thick fog rampantly swallowed up everything in its path, as it engulfed the whole surrounding area.

Unable to retreat, unable to run, Matthew, Catherine and Sam stood frozen. Thankfully at that moment the creeping, slithering, hunting living fog became still. Slowly it calmed down and settled softly like snow upon the ground.

The trees returned back to their lifeless being, their limp branches once again hung loosely down by their sides, their roots buried themselves deep into the life draining mud. Not a creak or moan could be heard, only the heavy breathing of Matthew, Sam and Catherine. Frightened of reawakening the fog, the three of them stood motionless.

Matthew poured with sweat. Catherine fought back her tears, and Sam gazed intently into the forest. The fog, slept.

Unfortunately however, it didn't settle for long. The relentless fog rose back to life, springing up high to create a thick towering wall. Matthew, Catherine and Sam watched on in awe. In the shape of a gigantic dam, the curved wall of fog revealed a small gap in which the darkness peered through.

Matthew's heart raced in his chest and his throat

tightened, but still he stood there staring through the gap, waiting in anticipation.

They didn't have to wait long before a deafening chorus of howls erupted out of the dam. The smell of death rushed more aggressively through the open gap.

"Wolf-lizards," Matthew whispered to himself, then suddenly realising his own words, he screamed out, "wolf-lizards!!"

"Now we're dead!" Catherine bellowed.

"Calm down you two, we have to remain quiet," Sam whispered trying to calm the two frightened youngsters.

"Calm down, how can you say that? They will kill us!" Catherine panicked.

"Listen to me, Catherine listen, we have to remain quiet, then with any luck they won't notice we're here. Wolf-lizards will only kill if they sense your fear, so calm down!"

But just as Matthew had feared, out of the unforgiving fog the sound of those deadly wolf-lizards howled.

"Shush, if we stay still they might not come through," Sam said trying her hardest to reassure Matthew and Catherine.

From the other side of the dam wall, they could

hear the monsters lifting their snout-like jaws up into the air, and sniffing in the night sky.

Then, another bout of howls rose up getting closer and closer. Hearing them sniffing their way along the other side of the fog wall, Matthew, Sam and Catherine could make out the wolf-lizard's shadows.

Sam lifted her finger to her lips, reminding them both to remain quiet, but those sensitive snouts weren't for giving up. Smelling the hint of sweat and fresh pounding blood, one by one the wolf-lizards poured through the gap.

Their bulging eyes filled with joy as they discovered hidden on the other side, three tasty treats.

A panicked stricken Sam ordered fearfully, "Quick, run!!"

The three of them set off racing through the forest, stumbling over broken tree branches and jumping over the reaching roots.

The howling of the wolf-lizards echoed through the sky, as the blood thirsty monsters rejoiced in their hunt. Shooting out their fiery tongues, red flames sparked against the baron trees, causing flashes of fire down around the three intruders.

"Quick, I know somewhere we can hide!" Sam spluttered, without question Catherine and Matthew followed.

Burying themselves deep down into the thick woodlands, the three of them tried to hide out of sight of the monsters.

"Matthew, I'm scared," Catherine whispered moving closer to Matthew.

Placing his arm around her he spoke, "I know, me too."

"Sam, where do you think they are?" Matthew asked clinging onto Catherine.

"I don't know? But maybe if we hide here for a bit they might get fed up!"

"Or they might feed up on us?" Matthew remarked back to Sam.

Being as quiet as they possibly could, they waited.

More howls echoed across the sky, followed by the sniffing of those deadly beasts. These creatures were hungry and were not for giving up easily.

"Listen," Sam finally spoke, "if we can get to the graveyard, we'll be safe."

"The graveyard? You didn't tell us about a graveyard!" Matthew asked.

Catherine looked up at him, "Matthew, I think it's a bit late to be questioning Sam on what we are doing here, or where we're heading. After all, this was your idea!"

"Look, whatever we need to do we can't do that

here," Sam whispered whilst pulling the light catcher out of her rucksack. The wolf-lizards lifted their snouts and howled angrily towards each other, with every small move the trio made.

Sam crept slowly out of their hiding place with the light catcher. Hoping to get a glimpse of where the wolf-lizards were waiting.

"Catherine, I'm sorry about all this, you do know that don't you?"

Looking down into her eyes, the feeling of guilt was almost overwhelming. Catherine innocently replied, "Of course I do."

Moments later Sam returned, "Well, the good news is," she whispered, "we don't have to go past the wolf-lizards."

"And the bad news?" Catherine asked sharply.

"The bad news is, we're going to have to make a run for it, quick follow me!"

Before Matthew and Catherine had chance to think about that thought, Sam was weaving herself in and out of the trees, leaving Catherine and Matthew no choice but to follow swiftly behind her.

Howling excitedly, the wolf-lizards then took up the chase once more. Their tongues whipped into the sky before slamming down with a thud.

"Faster!" Sam panted back.

"We are!" Catherine called.

The wolf-lizards were almost catching them. Matthew could feel their stale breaths touching the back of his neck, not wanting to look back, he kept focussed on Catherine.

"Arragh!" Matthew screamed, feeling the fiery deadly strike of a wolf- lizard's tongue. Knocking him face down into the mud, Matthew felt his back burning as the intense hot poison soaked deep into his skin.

"Sam! Matthew's been hit!" Catherine shouted turning to run back for him.

Managing to roll himself over, Matthew slowly shuffled back. The monsters stopped and growled at him. Shuffling away from them, their intense fire spread across his back and up towards his shoulders.

The wolf-lizards slithered closer towards him, viciously snapping their jaws, licking their deadly razor sharp teeth in anticipation of their food.

Catherine gazed on helpless, her heart was in her mouth, and tears filled her eyes. Sam, rather assuring given the situation, whispered in Catherine's ear, "Don't move until I say."

Swiftly Sam slid an arrow from her backpack and positioned it onto her bow, waiting for the right moment to strike.

The pack of wolf-lizards stared at one another

before one of them slithered over towards Matthew. With each move the wolf-lizard made, an accompanying howl of encouragement came from the blood thirsty creatures. With a sense of arrogance, the wolf-lizard looked Matthew up and down with its bulging black eyes, giving off a small growl and sneer. Then, another moment of arrogance made it reveal its deadly weapon. Emerging from its dagger like teeth, that fiery rotten fleshed tongue. Tilting its head backwards and pointing its tongue into the sky, with one swift movement it slammed it back down into the mud. The wolf-lizard then turned to its pack, and back once more to Matthew.

Suddenly, a high pitched whistling noise pierced through the clean still air. Matthew closed his eyes tightly. A fizzling sound shattered the air, followed by a sudden shuddering of the earth below.

Cautiously he opened his eyes. Matthew looked on astonished as the wolf-lizard's motionless body sprawled out across the mud. Its once deadly tongue was now hanging powerless from its mouth. Its flames were well and truly extinguished.

Now standing over Matthew, was Sam. Her eyes were as black as the night itself, searching through the dark, without speaking she ordered the wolf-lizards to retreat. Her face was narrow and washed free of colour.

Continuing to guard Matthew, she quickly prepared another arrow ready to fire. However, like whimpering dogs, the wolf-lizards scurried back through the dam. Darkmoor's monsters at last, were gone.

Catherine rushed over to Matthew, and placing her hands under his arms, she tried to haul him to his feet.

Looking up at her he asked, "Did you see, Catherine? Sam's eyes they were black."

"Never mind that we need to get you up," she said and with one almighty pull, Matthew stood observing Sam.

"You ok?" Sam looked at him, her eyes back to their usual state.

"Yeah I think so, what happened to your eyes, Sam? They were black."

"Black!" Sam said shocked, "No I think that's the shock making you confused."

"No I'm not confused, I know what I saw!" Matthew said raising his voice.

"Matthew it's ok, we're safe, that's all that matters," Catherine said softly.

"Catherine's right, and anyway, you should be thanking me, I just saved your life!" Sam said sarcastically with a small smirk across her face.

Walking over to the dead wolf-lizard, Sam pulled out her blood stained arrow, wiped it clean across her jeans, then looked back towards Catherine and Matthew, "Well, at least we have dinner!" she grinned.

Dear Diary,

Me, Matthew and Sam are sat round a camp fire which Sam has made. Dinner was good, roast wolf-lizard! I'm getting use to the fatty taste of it, actually it taste a bit like beef, only hairier!

Matthew was quiet over dinner. I think something's bothering him, but he won't say!

This forest is so creepy. Bugs are always crawling over me.

Anyway, Sam says we're going to rest here for tonight then move on tomorrow. She said something about a graveyard which leads us to Darkmoor's Castle. I just want to be home and safe in my own bed. I would give anything to hear my Mum and Dad again, warning me to stay away from that flipping vicarage. I wish I had now!

I really hope this plan of his works. For some stupid reason, Matthew thinks he will be able to talk to Darkmoor and somehow reason with him. Still, I suppose it's worth a shot, I'm just really praying it works.

Right well I'd better try and get some rest, Goodnight xxx

- Chapter Twelve -

Darkmoor's Graveyard

"The holiday just continues! You sure know how to treat a girl, Matthew!" Catherine signed sarcastically, as they made their way through the graveyard.

A pebbled path weaved around the grave stones, an old rotten railing barricaded the graveyard and the ever present fog circled slowly around the outer wall.

Bowing his head, Matthew's eyes were drawn to a name chiselled onto one of the solid headstones. He began to read them aloud, "Robert Peterson, Annabel Barrie, Sophie Mason-"

Sam abruptly interrupted, "Matthew, stop it, we don't need a running commentary!"

"No, no of course not, sorry" Matthew replied apologetically.

Visible across the graveyard was a metal rusty gate, which was swinging loosely on its hinges. This (as Sam had informed them) was the gateway to Darkmoor's castle, and although a huge volume of thick fog was keeping the castle from view, Matthew and Catherine trustingly followed her. Trudging along the path, Matthew couldn't avoid his eyes being drawn to the headstones, and quietly to himself he started reading the names again.

Coming to a sudden halt, he paused for a moment in disbelief. Then stepping off the path, he moved closer to one of the graves.

Reaching out his hand, he placed it onto the hard, cold slab and weaved his finger along the chiselled letters. A look of disbelief drew across his face, his heart sank and stomach turned. He repeated the same motion over and over again.

Glancing up towards the girls, who had now both stopped, Matthew slowly read the name out loud, "Samantha Harris."

Again Matthew repeated the name, "Samantha Harris."

Sam froze, but Matthew continued to read aloud the name.

"Stop it Matthew, just stop it!" Sam instructed, her voice bouncing off the headstone and rattling the railings. "Just stop!"

"That can't be you, Sam?" Matthew asked bewildered.

Without words, Sam sighed before nodding reluctantly.

"What!" Catherine gasped. "You're dead!"

"How can this be?" Matthew's anger filled voice boomed through the graveyard.

"You have a grave, you're dead," Catherine repeated shaking her head, vacantly looking at Matthew.

Ignoring Catherine's words, Sam stepped towards Matthew, but he moved away, "Don't touch me, don't come anywhere near me!"

"Look, I know this must look odd, but please Matthew, you have to trust me." Sam said softly trying to defuse the situation.

"Trust you! Who are you? This is your grave!!" Matthew shouted. His voice disturbed the calm fog as it arose from its pit.

"Matthew, look over there out of the fog, look!" Catherine called pointing towards the outer walls of the graveyard.

An eruption of wailing, screaming, and crying all blended into one depressing noise from within the fog.

Then one by one, out of the fog they crawled, like scavenging dogs hunting the next feast: zombie like creatures began to pursue the two youngsters. Covered in torn white rags which scraped along the mud, their empty hollow eyes stared intently towards them. Each blood hunting zombie growled with gnashing fang-like teeth. Droplets of blood dripped from their mouths. An uncountable number of them lined up on the other side before clambering over the rotten railings.

"What is this place?" Matthew said throwing Sam a killer look.

"I really want to go home now Matthew," a tearful Catherine said.

"You two need to get out of here!" Sam ordered them whilst positioning an arrow onto her bow, "I will keep them here, Darkmoor wants you Matthew, so go!"

Suddenly, just the mention of his name made Matthew feel dizzy, and the torturous sounds of the graveyard began to fade away.

I am standing here, at the river bank, trying to find somewhere to cross. The fog is all around me, and it's making my body cold. I can hear her voice calling for me, "Catherine, I'm coming" I shout in the hope of reassuring her, but I can still hear her cries.

He's here. Darkmoor's here. Standing in front of me looking down at me, then he lifts his head up towards the sky and lets out a caw!

I have to save Catherine, I have to defeat him, I have to...

"Matthew, run!" Sam ordered again bringing

Matthew back round from his trance. Not needing to be told a third time, Matthew grabbed Catherine's arm and headed for the exit gate.

"Come on, we're not dying here today!" Matthew promised.

Running past the headstones they eventually reached the castle's gateway. Matthew took one more glance across the now living graveyard as Sam fired piercing arrows from her bow.

Like a battle field, only with sinister zombies, Sam stood like a soldier on the front line, ready for battle.

"We can't just leave her Catherine," Mathew said.

"Yes we can, you heard her and besides she's already dead, remember!"

Sensing Matthew and Catherine were still watching, Sam barked another order, "You two get out of here… now!!"

"Well you heard her Matthew, let's go," Catherine said gripping tightly hold of Matthew's hand. Together they turned and forced open the crooked gate.

They leapt into the swirling fog, which wrapped , as quickly as it had formed, the fog rapidly evaporated.

"Oh my," Catherine gasped, her jaw dropped and her eyes widened.

The graveyard had completely vanished and silence

had fallen. They stood completely alone on the moors of Darkmoor's land.

Stretched upwards before them, were about a hundred stone steps which sank into the climbing hillside. Nervously, Matthew looked up towards the top of the hill. Perched high in top was a medieval castle.

"Well I'm guessing this is it?" Matthew said looking down at Catherine, who looked amazed at the medieval palace.

"Yeah I think your right," Catherine replied.

The steps in front of them led up to the entrance which was a stone archway, situated centrally on the front wall. The castle was battered, weathered and worn. Tiny pieces of stone occasionally broke free, bouncing off the walls before crashing down the hillside. Small rectangular stone windows were scattered randomly around the castle, each one aglow with what seemed like flickering candlelight.

Four protruding circle stone towers hugged the outer crumbling walls. Bats darted in between the turrets and around the castle's flagpole. At first glance the flag looked completely black, but as the wind died, the flag hung still, and its picture was that of a crow.

The air around them grew colder, and overhead a thumping thunder clattered and crashed, followed shortly by ripples of lightning, which shot down around the hillside, highlighting the castles battle scars.

"Caw, caw," that call sent a shiver down Matthew's spine. Protectively he grabbed Catherine. Crow called again.

Matthew breathed heavy and gazed up towards the top of the castle. Proudly perched perfectly on top of the flagpole, was the all too Clever Crow.

"There you are," Matthew uttered under his breath.

His smooth coat sparkled majestically in the stormy moonlight. His beady eyes eagerly watched his two tiny intruders below. This was Crow's castle, Crow's home, and no one was moving in uninvited.

Crow opened up his powerful wings and effortlessly hopped up into the raging sky. Wonderfully he camouflaged himself against the black backdrop of the night sky. Only glimmers of moonlight gave away his splendour.

Letting out a caw, the crow spiralled above his castle, all the while watching Matthew and Catherine. Knowing he had their full attention, he swooped down momentarily out of sight behind the castle's walls. Then, gathering speed, Crow shot back up into the sky and disappeared. Crow was gone.

"Where do you think he's gone?" Catherine asked nervously.

"Probably in the castle waiting," Matthew replied. "Are you ready?" Matthew added confidentially without looking at Catherine, but keeping his eye's fixed on the castle.

She swallowed hard and just about managed to answer, "I think so."

This was it, it was now or never. Knowing that he must face whatever was hidden behind the castle walls, bravely they started to climb the long stone steps, ever closer, towards Darkmoor's castle.

- Chapter Thirteen -

Darkmoor revealed

With every step, Matthew could feel his heart drumming inside his chest.

"You ok, Catherine?" Matthew asked, as Catherine walked nervously behind him breathing heavily. All the while they watched anxiously for Crow to reappear.

"Yeah," she replied. Clearly she was petrified, but she'd gotten use to getting on with things.

When they had almost reached the top step, the hillside seemed to drift further and further away.

Finally, they reached the open archway. Walking through the cobbled alley way, the smell of damp drifted in the air, and at the far end of the alley shone a bright blinding light. Allowing the light to lead them, they continued.

Upon reaching the end of the alley, the glowing light brightened, revealing more and more of this dangerous place.

Before long, Matthew and Catherine found

themselves stood centre stage in an open aired Roman-like theatre. Above them a roof of night spanned across.

"What the!" Matthew gasped.

"I don't like this Matthew," Catherine shivered.

Just then, the theatre became aglow with fierce candlelight, only this time it wasn't a warming glow, but an angry flicker. As the light reflected off the surrounding walls, it truly revealed how vast the space around them was.

"What is this place?" Matthew muttered darting his eyes around the theatre.

Dotted around were thick stone pillars, each one reaching up into the sky. Surrounding Matthew and Catherine, in a horse shoe shape, stone tiers climbed several hundred feet, until the dark sky swallowed the tops of them.

"I think we should leave, we should never have come here without Sam," Catherine warned, looking desperately at Matthew.

He looked down at her fear filled eyes. He knew, deep down, that this was an almost impossible mission, but also deep down he knew that it would have to be made possible. An inward battle took place in Matthew's head. The wiser appeared to be cautious as Matthew agreed with Catherine.

Turning to run back down the alley, a ruffled croaky voice spoke out of the darkness, "Don't forget me."

A long thin dark shadow accompanied that somewhat familiar voice. From within the alley emerged a figure and the candlelight lit up her face. Lifting her hand to wave towards them, she silently mouthed, "Hello."

"Sam!" Catherine called, and before Matthew had chance to stop her, she rushed over towards a weary Sam. Managing to find the energy, she embraced Catherine tightly.

"Hi Matthew, don't I get a hug from you?" Sam asked her voice still sounding raw. "Are you not glad to see me?" Sam asked whilst squeezing Catherine harder.

"Ok Sam," Catherine began, trying to pull herself away from Sam's hold, "you can let go now, please you're hurting me!"

Sam didn't respond, rather she was focusing her burning eyes deep into Matthew.

"Sam, let her go!" Matthew ordered sternly. He could feel his hand starting to throb, but this time he would not let the pain overcome him.

"I said let her go!" Matthew shouted again.

Upon raising his voice, Sam's eyes flashed black. Her voice grew deeper, "You fool Matthew. Did you really think it would be this easy?" Looking up towards the stormy sky, Sam threw her head back and out of her roared an evil laughter.

As Sam released Catherine from her grip, Matthew rushed over to her and protectively hunched over her.

The castle began to shake violently, Sam's laughter filled the theatre and above them an almighty storm broke out, sending rain hammering into the arena.

The white fog awakened and crawled its way through the alleyway, wrapping itself around Sam, cocooning her body and lifting her up into the sky.

Letting out another evil bellow of laughter, the thunder roared in approval and gave out an electric bolt which battered the castle walls.

"Let's get out," Matthew shouted trying to help Catherine to her feet. "Come on!"

Dragging Catherine to her feet, they sprinted with all their might towards the exit.

The storm came to an abrupt halt and retreated. Catherine and Matthew's relentless misery continued, as the sound of howls rang throughout Darkmoor. Gradually getting louder, the howls echoed off the storm damaged walls. Then one by one, marching through the alleyway came Darkmoor's monstrous army.

"We're dead this time!" Catherine cried, nodding towards the wolf-lizards.

"Catherine, come here," Matthew spoke quietly reaching out for her hand.

The wolf-lizards circled a petrified Matthew and Catherine. They slammed their fiery tongues down onto the slab floor and the theatre shuddered. Their rotten stale breath breathed onto the youngsters, and salvia dripped uncontrollably from their jaws. Their bulging black eyes filled with delight as they eagerly anticipated their long over due feast. Then another bout of howls erupted around the theatre as the wolf-lizards grew in excitement.

"**Silentium!**" a voice ordered, immediately causing the wolf-lizards to stand upright. Matthew recognised that all too familiar voice. It had tortured him, caused him pain; it had been a constant voice inside his head and now it was more real than ever. The blood underneath Matthew's skin bubbled up with anger. The wolf-lizards looked at each other. Matthew knew exactly who that deep, smooth raw voice belonged to.

A deafening silence fell, without instruction the wolf-lizard's parted. A tall slim shadow stretched over the theatre floor. Matthew looked up, firstly seeing black boots coated with mud, then a long black coat swaying from side to side. Matthew looked further up the figure, his heart racing, his throat closing, sensing those black steely eyes fixed firmly upon him. Matthew rose to his feet, ready to face the man of his nightmares.

Not being disappointed, there he stood. His face was narrow and gaunt, his long black sleek hair cascading freely down over his broad shoulders.

"Darkmoor," Matthew whispered.

Stepping through the mesmerised monsters, Darkmoor spoke arrogantly, "So Matthew, we do meet again."

"Yeah, I guess so," Matthew spoke.

"And Catherine, my beautiful Catherine, the one I watched grow up," Darkmoor spoke more calmly and smoothly now, and he reached out his hand to stroke Catherine's face. Matthew quickly smacked it away.

"Don't touch her!" he said assertively.

Tilting his head, Darkmoor narrowed his gaze upon Matthew, "Did you really think you could defeat me? Do you know how long I have been waiting for you?"

"Who are you? What do you want with us?" Matthew demanded.

"Well," Darkmoor began whilst lifting his hands up into the air, "I am Darkmoor, master of the dark, master of all tricks and master of my land." His words sent a shiver down Matthew's spine.

"Where is Sam, what have you done with her?" Catherine asked.

"My darling Catherine, are you really that stupid? Have you not worked it out?" Then looking back at Catherine and Matthew, Darkmoor continued, "I am Sam, did you really think she was capable of talking to my beautiful angels in the river, or stopping my monsters from killing you both in the woods?"

"No! It was all you!" Catherine cried in disbelief.

"Yes my dear, it was all me. I am the crow, I am the old man and yes I am Sam. It's all very clever don't you think?"

"When you were the old man, you said you knew my mother. How do you know her?" Matthew puzzled.

"Your mother," Darkmoor voice filled with anger at the mention of her name, "your mother boy is the one who put me here, wel,l she the one that made me get so angry that I created this place. I loved her, but she, she tricked me into believing she loved me, do you see!?" Darkmoor stated expecting Matthew to understand.

"No, my mother was a good person she would never have done this!" Matthew shouted as he could feel his temper bubbling up inside.

"Your mother, ha, you didn't even know her. She

played us both, but I loved her not him, not Jack-"

"Wait my dad, you mean my dad?" Matthew asked.

Darkmoor aimed his fiery stare towards Matthew.

"You boy, you will never understand!" His voice was raw, steely and cold. Angry flashed in his eyes and lifting his hands up into the air, Darkmoor clapped them twice.

Automatically the wolf-lizards began to circle Matthew and Catherine once more.

"Kill the girl, but the boy...the boy is mine!" Darkmoor ordered, his eyes furiously burning through Matthew.

The wolf-lizards grunted, rejoicing at the command.

"No!" Catherine screamed.

- Chapter Fourteen -

It's only just begun

"No Catherine!!" Matthew shouted, however his words were drowned out by the sound of the roaring beasts.

Catherine's scream screeched throughout the theatre, "No, I don't want to die! Matthew!"

Looking towards Darkmoor, Matthew pleaded, "Kill me instead, it's me you want!"

Darkmoor's deadly black eyes darted towards him.

"Don't you understand, Matthew? I need you alive, Catherine was the bait to get you here." Then Darkmoor let out a roar of laughter before continuing, "Master of tricks, I tell you fool."

Stepping closer to Mathew, Darkmoor looked at the wolf-lizards and smiled, "They're hungry you see, I couldn't let them eat you in the forest, I wanted you alive, but Catherine," tilting his head, Darkmoor looked at her then back at Matthew, "she looks tasty don't you think?"

"Please Darkmoor, please!" Again Matthew pleaded, but his words were ignored. "Please I'm begging you, she doesn't deserve to die!" Matthew shouted.

"Believe me Matthew, to have you killed as well would give me great pleasure, but after waiting ten years for you to come, I'm not going to let you go that easy," Darkmoor said wickedly.

"Why? What do you need me for? Who are you?" Matthew demanded again, hoping to get some kind of explanation, but Darkmoor turned his back and encouraged the hungry wolf-lizards to feed.

"No!" Matthew cried looking on at a helpless Catherine, who was hunched over on the floor.

As Matthew's voice spiralled up in the night sky, suddenly a blinding white light streamed over the crumbling castle walls. Filtering down through the theatre, it caused the wolf-lizards to stop their torturing, and immediately they dropped to the floor.

"No!" Darkmoor whined covering his eyes to block out the powerful light.

Unaffected by the light, Matthew looked up towards the top of the castle. Sat perfectly still upon one of the towers, was Dove. Beautiful, glorious, radiant light spiralled down from her wings, illuminating the darkness.

With a graceful flutter, she lifted herself up into the sky. Swooping down towards Matthew, Dove released a protective fairy dust blanket over him.

Dove glided peacefully towards Matthew. She was double his size, and her white calming eye's smiled softly at him. Instantly the fear of Darkmoor washed away, and allowing himself to be wrapped up in Dove's angelic wings, she cocooned Matthew into safety. Dove tilted her head and gently flapped her wing, taking Matthew to the calm sky above and out over the castle walls.

Dove's lightness faded and darkness returned. Darkmoor looked up at the calm sky and grunted. Clouds gathered above and a trace of fairy dust danced in the night sky.

"No! That flaming Dove!"

Turning back towards a whimpering Catherine, who was still hunched over on the theatre floor, he angrily commanded, "Throw her into the dungeons, he'll come back for her. Then I will kill him!"

'My head ... my head is throbbing!'

I can feel the ground is soft underneath me, warm and soft. I slowly open my eyes.

"What?" I'm back in my bedroom, quickly I jump to my feet. The sunlight is pouring in through the grubby old

windows, that lovely homely smell of dirt, damp, dust and rot lingers through the air.

'Was it all a dream?' I think to myself whilst looking down at my hand. The cut from Crow's razor shape beak has completely vanished, not even a scar is present.

Not taking any chances I quickly flash my eyes along every tree branch, thankfully that clever crow is nowhere to be seen.

'It seemed so real, but it can't have been.'

A faint knocking at the door interrupts me from my thought. Suddenly, I hear my Dad speak, so quickly I jump to my feet and race towards the top of the stone staircase.

"Hello," Dad's voice says softly, then sure enough another person's response.

Breathing out a sigh of relief, I wait eagerly, anticipating Catherine's voice. I wait, and wait, and wait, but nothing.

'What are they talking about?' I wonder.

Slowly making my way down the staircase, Pete and Julie come into view. Reaching the bottom step I notice my Dad's back turned towards me, and his head is hanging down towards the floor.

As I step closer I realise that Julie is crying, whilst Pete is reassuring her that it's going to be ok.

'What will be ok?' I begin to wonder. Before I have chance to ask, my Dad slams the door shut, places some sort of leaflet on the sideboard and walks past me shaking his head.

Without exchanging words, I curiously look down at the glossy paper.

"Catherine…" I whisper as I feel tears fill my eyes, "Catherine!" I shout out as my legs give way beneath me, once more the pain of Crow becomes ever present, and my hand begins to angrily throb. Deep red blood begins to pulsate breaking my skin, and as I grip the paper with Catherine's face on, tears stream down my face. In disbelief I read the bold writing again,

"10 year old Catherine Rose went missing four days ago at a car boot sale!"

I sit myself down on the cold hallway floor. Minutes pass.

Something moves. I anxiously glance towards the steps. There's nothing there. I stare at the floor. It's there again. The floor creaks and I look up to find a shadow cast on the landing above. I hit myself on the cheek to awaken myself, but I am awake. Another creak follows then an all too familiar outline of Crow. Pure fear overwhelms me, he's calling me, gloating, reminding me that it wasn't a dream after all.

'I know it's not over,' I think to myself as his evil caw bellows out across the whole of Filius, and throughout the old Victorian vicarage.